How would you react if you found yourself on a modern day Noah's Ark (with no foreseeable prospect of finding dry land)?

What could you think of to extend the limited supply of food?

Would you agree to separate sleeping quarters for male and female?

Would you feel that any human life you encountered was precious to the survival of the race, or would you want to kill all others in order to give yourself a better chance?

How would you survive?

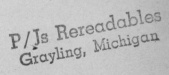

AFTER THE RAIN

by
JOHN BOWEN

BALLANTINE BOOKS • NEW YORK

Library of Congress Catalog Card No. 58-11034

First printing   January 1959
Second printing   August 1965

Printed in the United States of America

Ballantine Books, Inc., 101 Fifth Avenue,
New York, N. Y. 10003

for my
Mother and Father

Inky pinky spider, climbing up the spout,
Down came the rain, and washed poor spider out.
Out came the sun, and dried away the rain.
Inky pinky spider, climbing up again.

Children's nursery rhyme

AFTER THE RAIN

1. The Rain-Maker

There are no beginnings in history; all that belongs to pre-history and imagination. Chains of events and ideas stretch backwards and forwards through time, and can be traced in either direction by people who have a fancy for that sort of thing, but traced to no beginnings, and each end is a different question mark.

History is too big for beginnings that we can apprehend, but men are not big. Men are small, and each man has a beginning when he is conceived, an end when he dies; the before and after of those events are not comprehensible by his understanding, and so have no part in his life as a man. And, just as each man has his own beginning, so the chain of events and ideas of which I have spoken have a beginning for him; that is the moment when they come within his own personal experience.

So that, while for some folk the Flood began at the seventh (eighth? ninth? thirtieth?) day of steady rain, for others only when the level of the water reached the top of the television set or the turkey carpet, for still others at that very moment when the water itself reached out for them to overwhelm them with cold and suffocation, for me it began in the basement of Foyle's Book Shop in the Charing Cross Road, almost a year before Mr. Uppingham detonated whatever it was he detonated, and covered the earth in rain.

The Book Buying Department was in Foyle's basement. A little counter was set off from the girls who sorted or despatched the new books that lay about in profusion elsewhere in the basement, and behind this counter there was a room to the right where the Buyer lived when he

9

was not buying, along with the confidential dusty catalogues that told him whether a textbook was out of date or not. He seemed to me an incongruously cheerful man. I always expected a Buyer to be sympathetically depressed; so many of his clients had come down in the world.

He was a very useful barometer, that Buyer. I could tell which literary reputations were still sound as I watched him going through a suitcase of eighteenth- and nineteenth-century authors, discarding perhaps a third of the books. "No good taking Scott nowadays," he would say cheerfully, "Bulwer Lytton?—oh, my dear chap! George Eliot—we get that kind of stuff by the ton. Froude . . . Grote— What a lot of copies Everyman must have printed of Grote! Dickens, yes. Trollope, yes. Peacock, yes. Fielding, yes—oh no; it's Amelia, I'm afraid. Not Thackeray. Not Smollet. Not Gissing. I'll give you twenty-five shillings for the lot."—and so they would begin a journey through whatever processes were necessary before they reached their final end on the Sixpenny Shelf.

I was selling review copies to Foyle's at that time, and went pretty regularly to the Buying Department every fortnight or so, and I grew to recognize most of the other regular clients. I myself was of the aristocracy; all the books I brought were new, and I had a good price for them. This put me in a class with the elderly Kensington lady in a purple hat, who used to come in with a string bag full of detective stories, which she had bought to read and sell again; books from the libraries, she said, were full of germs. I remember that I once told her that even Foyle's books were handled by somebody before she bought them, but she said that one found a better class of customer at Foyle's than the people who went to libraries.

Below this lady and myself in the scale there were the students in corduroys with Oxford histories and textbooks on mathematics. Below them were those who were students no longer—middle-aged folk in reduced circum-

interspersed with joke drawings and unintentionally comic bits cut out of other magazines. Our critics wrote of the Arts in a tone of urbane irritation, and we laid great stress on features distinguished for their objective reporting; I had been hired as one of the objective reporters at a flat salary of fifteen pounds a week. As it happened, Londoners who liked that kind of thing continued to subscribe to *The New Yorker*, and our magazine barely lasted a year. It folded, in fact, a couple of months after my meeting with Mr. Uppingham, and was mourned at great length ("the contraction of any market at all for good writing", "the imminent death of the little magazines", the menace of television") by those people who might have saved it by buying the magazine instead of whining about it after it was gone. However, they were paid for their elegies, I suppose, whereas a subscription to *North Latitude* would have cost three guineas a year.

It had been my thought that Mr. Uppingham might serve as copy for our "On the Spot" columns, as indeed he did to the tune of four long paragraphs under the heading "Undampened", which began, "It was our pleasure yesterday to drink coffee with a professional rain-maker," and ended, "Water polo, anyone?" I sent a copy of these paragraphs, together with my own much longer version of the story, to a friend who knew the Science Editor of the *News Chronicle*, and landed a job as a Special Correspondent, accompanying Mr. Uppingham to Texas.

The principle on which the State of Texas engaged Mr. Uppingham was simple: it couldn't do any harm to try him, and he would not be paid unless he were successful. A certain number of inches of rain must fall within two days of the conclusion of his attempt; the State of Texas had had truck with rain-makers before. The principle on which Mr. Uppingham proposed to make the rain was just as simple in its essence, but much more difficult to understand. "Ay dare say," he had explained at that first meeting, "Ay dare say you did Chemistry at school?"

"Yes."

"And Ay dare say you remember that if you pass a direct current through water bay means of electrodes, haidrogen collects around one electrode and oxygen around the other. Twaice as much haidrogen as oxygen."

"Yes."

"Well, there you are."

"Where am I?"

"If you can turn water into haidrogen and oxygen—into air, dear boy, do you see?—all you have to do is reverse the process, and you have water again."

"But how?"

"What is lightning, dear boy, if it is not Nature's own version of this process?"

I stopped to take thought. "Lightning doesn't have any electrodes," I said, "and it doesn't go on for long enough. Anyway, lightning isn't always accompanied by rain; I'm sure I've heard of dry lightning. And even when it is, the rain often comes first."

"Exactly. Ay have often had occasion to say it; Nature is deplorably unscayentific. What is required, dear boy, for any scayentific process is control."

"Just control?"

"And a catalyst. The only contribution you might say Ay have made is the discovery of a catalyst."

"And what is it?"

"May dear boy," said Mr. Uppingham, "if Ay were to tell you that, it would make you as rich as Ay hope to become mayself."

He wouldn't tell me. He woudn't tell anyone what his catalyst was. The whole thing was preposterous. He had bought for his Texan experiment (from some dump of surplus stores, I assume) a small barrage balloon, and he adapted it secretly to his purposes. He filled it with hydrogen and oxygen in the proportions of two to one, and added some of his catalyst; whether it was gas, liquid or solid, nobody knew. Then he discovered that the balloon would not leave the ground. By this time he was getting a great deal of rather frivolous publicity, and holidaymakers began to flock to the scene of his experiment. I believed, and still do, that Mr. Uppingham was not as stupid as we made out, because it was discovered at that point that he had rented a large area of the ground round about his "construction shed, fifteen miles north of Cisco, Texas, and he now made money by selling concessions to the hot-dog, hamburger and soft drink stalls that sprang up near the shed for the service of the tourists whose numbers increased every day. Even if the experiment itself were to be a failure, Mr. Uppingham was pretty sure to make by these methods a sum considerably greater than his expenses.

He set to work again on the balloon, attaching to the top of it a helicopter blade, which was to be driven by a motor that he would carry with him in the basket. This motor would also supply the current needed for the electrolysis. Mr. Uppingham himself intended to be in the basket to start the process going, and watch developments. The theory was that, once the process had begun, valves would open at each end of the balloon, rain being expelled as a spray from one valve, while fresh quantities of air were drawn in through the other; this would not be as pure as the artificial "air" used to start the process, but it would do. The balloon, tethered by cable to a lorry, would move about shedding its spray of rain all over the state, and from the lorry food and drink would be sent up to Mr. Uppingham, and petrol for the motor.

Now that I have explained all this in detail, you may imagine the kind of articles that flip journalists were writing about Mr. Uppingham. Cisco filled up with the feature-writers of American and European periodicals. Punch sent a peer, and Paris-Match a husband-and-wife team. Money filled the tills of the bars and drug stores of Cisco and its neighbouring townships. Hotels and rooming houses had never had it so good; whether he made any rain or not, the local citizens had cause to thank Mr. Uppingham. As I have said, I myself never

believed at the time he intended getting more than the
profits from the concessions he had sold, with the added
possibility of selling his life story afterwards to some national magazine.

The Uppingham Story ended on the 8th of August 1965.
The morning was fine and clear, with the usual prospect of baking heat to come; that part of Texas had been
without rain for nine years, and the vegetable covering
of the earth had been withered away by the sun. All the
correspondents and agency photographers were stirring
early in Cisco that morning, for the balloon was to go
up at eleven o'clock. I had been luckier in my lodgings
than most, for I was staying with the mother of an old
friend from the days I had spent at Indiana University,
and, after a breakfast of orange juice, coffee, and scrambled
eggs, with bacon grilled until it was brittle and dried on
crepe paper, I walked out to join my breakfastless col-
leagues at the site of the shed, stepping delicately among
the little town of tents and trailers that had grown up
around it. There we waited with the ever-growing crowd
until Mr. Uppingham appeared at ten.

The balloon was no more than a collapsed sheath of
silk on the truck; a State Trooper guarded it, and swapped
jokes with some of the people close to him. Another truck
was parked at a little distance away; it contained the
cylinders of gas with which the balloon was to be filled.
Mr. Uppingham ordered this second truck into position,
and began to superintend the operation.

As before, the balloon did not at once leave the truck
to which it was attached by cable, but only took on shape
as the cylinders of gas were emptied. This was a slow
business, and the crowd grew bored. They stood about
and shouted to their wandering children, or they sat on
cushions on the tops of automobiles and trailers, and
conversed with one another over the heads of the people
on the ground. Most of them were lightly dressed, and
all of them were sweating in the strong sun, which, as

the *putt-a-putt* of the motor sounded thinly in the air and the balloon began to rise beneath the rotating helicopter blade was suddenly obscured, so that everyone fell silent, and looked up.

It was not the balloon, of course, which had obscured the sun; that, though rising steadily, was still too close to the truck. No, a large cloud had come up from the west, and as Mr. Uppingham stepped into the basket, and as the cable was paid out and the balloon rose higher and higher into the air, other clouds came and joined the first, covering the sky like a padded quilt, and blotting out the sun. All time seemed to slow down as Mr. Uppingham rose in his basket towards the cloud quilt above him, which, as it grew thicker, seemed to come down to meet the balloon.

On the roof of one of the trailers, a trap door opened as a child was sent to fetch its mother's wrap. Suddenly the air grew chilly, and a shiver seemed to run through the crowd. A car was seen to drive furiously up the road from Cisco, and the people on foot made room for it, since it bore some sort of official pennant. The car stopped by the truck, and a middle-aged man in a light suit and a wide hat got out, and spoke sharply to the man at the winch. "Get him down," he said, "the deal's off."

"Don't know as how I could do that," said the man.

"The deal's off."

"Does he know?" The man at the winch pointed into the air, where Mr. Uppingham could be seen, a tiny figure looking down at the people.

"O.K. I'll tell him." The middle-aged man made a megaphone of his hands, and shouted upwards to Mr. Uppingham. "Can you hear me? The deal's off. OFF. It is going to rain in any case. THE DEAL IS OFF." High above him, Mr. Uppingham smiled, and waved a benison from the basket.

Then, I suppose, he threw the switch. There was no sudden flash, nothing spectacular. It was just that the balloon seemed to disintegrate, and the basket and the helicopter blade hung there for a moment, two specks in the middle air, and then dropped. The basket hit the roof of one of the automobiles, belonging to a Mr. Henry Denton of Dallas, and smashed completely with Mr. Uppingham and all that was in it. The blade fell harmlessly on the ground.

A bustle and hubbub arose among the crowd, as its centre of interest shifted from the air above to its own midst, and the people re-formed into a new pattern that reflected this shift in focus, pressing closely around Mr. Denton's automobile. Then the State Troopers began to disperse them. The damaged automobile with its horrid discolouration on the roof, was taken over and driven away. One by one the tents and trailers vanished from the site, until only a litter of pop bottles, cans and papers was left to mark it. The site was deserted, and, by six in the evening, most of the correspondents and sight-seeing folk had left Cisco itself to renew the sleepy life of a small town.

At seven, the rain began.

2. The Face of the Earth

The rain began, and did not stop. A counterpane of cloud covered the U.S.A., Canada and the South American countries. It crossed the Atlantic and Pacific Oceans, and fell on Europe, Asia, Africa, Australia and the Arctic and Antarctic Circles. All over the world, the sun was blotted out, and the rain fell steadily.

Meteorologists, finding that their weather charts had now become absurdly simple, were left with nothing to predict. Such a thing, it was announced, had not happened before; there were no precedents for this sort of weather, and they could make no forecasts. The announcement provoked angry letters from low-Church fundamentalists who asked whether the Weather Bureaux had never heard of Noah. Other correspondents blamed the hydrogen bomb. But even the fundamentalists did not regard the rain as anything but a warning—after all, the Lord had promised that there would never be another Flood—and nobody expected it to go on for much longer.

The rain fell. Wheat, which is usually ready for harvesting in England in late August, rotted in the fields. Fresh vegetables became scarce in the shops, and rose alarmingly in price. As food prices rose, there was a burst of strikes. Dockers, miners and railwaymen, appalled at the increased cost of living, struck for higher wages, and the cost of living rose accordingly. Thomas Renton, an ex-postman living on a pension in Putney, committed suicide at about this time, and left a note for the coroner, laying out neatly in blue and red ink the details of his weekly budget. The tabloid and humanitarian newspapers made a big issue out of Mr. Renton's suicide letter, and the head of a well-known firm of publishers immediately began a campaign for the relief of the Elderly and Indigent.

A sudden rush of water, caught and stored in the Exmoor peat, swept away the little Devonshire town of Lynmouth, and the Lord Mayor of London sponsored a fund for the survivors. But, as similar catastrophes grew more frequent, the Lord Mayor's Fund became something of a joke. Although swelled by Government grants, the money and woolly clothing collected always seemed to be several catastrophes behind.

Now Noahs began to proliferate in Britain. There was a Plymouth Noah, a Bradford Noah, and a mad old man who lived just outside Luton. These were the first, and they had most publicity, but many others followed them, crying Woe at the sins of the world, and all of them making, with different degrees of skill, arks into which they proposed to cram themselves, their families and as many animals as they could come by. The Luton Noah was prosecuted for stealing sheep; the Plymouth Noah put out to sea, and was lost without trace; the Bradford Noah worked to the dimensions and materials laid down in the Bible, and never finished his ark for want of cypress. Many of the later Noahs found that the animals ate the grain they had gathered for planting on Ararat; wooden arks warped or, river-launched, were smashed to pieces against the parapet of some bridge. In spite of these misfortunes, the longer it rained, the more Noahs there were, though it became increasingly difficult to build an ark with one's home half under water, and no food in the larder to stock it.

I have written so far of how things were in Britain. Though I must have read in the newspapers of the early disasters in Holland and Connecticut, they are no more to me now than faded brown pictures in the *Illustrated London News*. It is our own misfortunes I remember. December was the turning month, for December brought freezing weather to Britain. The rain turned to snow, the flooded fields to ice. Planes were earth-bound; trains ran slowly and infrequently; buses, cars and vans clanked about in chains. Attendances at factories and offices fell away, and the people stayed at home (and for the most part in bed) fireless and hungry. The London County Council organized a service of vans that brought one hot meal a day to old people, but, even so, many of them died. So did the pigeons in Trafalgar Square.

The snow piled up in the streets of the towns. In the Highlands of Scotland, in North Wales and on the moors of England, communities were cut off from their neighbours, and, again, many people died and many cattle and sheep. Newspapers could no longer be nationally distributed, and were put out in skimpy local editions. As the country roads clogged up, food and other essentials were transported by helicopter, but the strain was too great for the service to be more than scratchily maintained, nor could the helicopters carry coal and firing. In London, snow-ploughs cleared the main highways, but the snow was piled up all the deeper in side streets, and there were clashes between tenant and tenant as basement-dwellers tried to move upstairs. Snow-shoes were sold out of the shops, and people learned to tramp about on tennis racquets and flat pieces of plywood.

In late February the thaw came. All over the country, swollen rivers burst their banks, bridges were carried away, farmhouses were inundated, and many more of those cattle and people who had survived the winter were drowned. The streets of London were under water. The crematoria of Golders Green and Woking worked overtime; they had been given the highest fuel priority, for the dead could not be buried. Now, with no crops planted or able to be planted, with communications cut and wide areas of the country under water, the Government proclaimed a State of Emergency.

After my return from Texas, I had left the staff of the News Chronicle to join an advertising agency in Mayfair. I was a copywriter. As the rain continued, and the snow followed it, our copy became more and more "flood-conscious"—"Get flood-conscious copywise," one of the directors told me, and an account executive nearby said, "Surely, surely!" I was concerned to sell, not the raincoats, gum-boots and all the various forms of water-proofing that people were already buying without encouragement, but the luxury articles that nobody in his senses would want during an emergency. It was all a little like a *New Statesman and Nation* competition. "STOCKING A RAFT?" I wrote, "Remember OYSTERS! Succulent and easily digested, Buxtable OYSTERS carry a lot of nourishment in a little space. They give you those RESERVES OF ENERGY you are going to NEED. OYSTERS in your provision box are worth their weight in PEARLS. Ask your grocer for BUX-TABLE'S BOTTLED OYSTERS now before it's too late."

I wrote copy about barometers ("FIRST WITH THE GOOD NEWS"), diamond necklaces ("SO LIGHT, SO HANDY, SO EASY TO CARRY"), and for Ford cars with the new rustless finish. I advertised sun-glasses ("SNOW GLARE ATTACKS THE EYES"), and suggested a campaign for a sun-tan cosmetic with the catch-line, "If you LOOK FIT, you ARE FIT." One selling scheme of mine proposed that parasols turned upside down could be filled with food and towed behind boats in flooded areas, but it was rejected as far-fetched.

As the winter wore on, and the national papers were restricted to a local circulation, we expected to lose accounts, but advertisers continued to buy space just the same. In times of adversity, "Business as Usual" is more than a boast; it is a refusal to believe that adversity exists. I continued to write copy of one sort and another until the thaw, by which time, newspapers, magazines, advertising agencies, commercial television, cinemas and indeed most businesses of any kind had closed down altogether for want of staff and the materials of production.

Hunger and disease were everywhere, but most, it seemed, in London. There were stories of cannibalism in the East End, and looting in Hampstead, Highgate and Notting Hill, where the streets were not yet under water. Over much of the rest of London, the streets had become canals, and not many of the gangs of looters had floating transport, for all sorts of boats and rubber dinghies had been commandeered by the Disposal Service. This was a kind of extension of the police, swollen by a recruitment of Special Constables and Civil Defence Volunteers, devoted to the protection of the public, both from violence and plague. They maintained a round-the-clock service—silent armed men in those absurd dinghies, jostled by the bodies which bobbed in the water, and which they collected and towed away to improvised crematoria.

Since my return I had been renting a room from Bob Humphries, an old school-fellow who was a member of the Disposal Service, and, now that I had little to do with my time, he often allowed me to accompany him on duty. It kept me from boredom, and by then I no longer cared whether I was indoors or out; being wet had become a condition of life, for there was almost no heating, and one's bedding and clothes were permanently damp. The natives of Tierra del Fuego, I had been told at school, endured this sort of existence; if they managed to get used to it, I supposed we should. I remember making this remark to Bob one morning as we paddled in convoy along the King's Road. The rain fell steadily, and, since the Disposal Service was already beginning to be a little behind in getting rid of the bodies, there was a pervading stench of decay. Suddenly Bob said, "It can't go on, you know."

"I wish I believed that."

"There's no sense to it." He stopped paddling, and stared at me earnestly. "I wish I had a cigarette," he said. Supplies of cigarettes and tobacco had given out long ago, and most of us had grown used to being without, but Bob, I think, since he had a request to make, had wanted to be able to offer me a cigarette. "I want you to do something for me, John," he said, "if you will."

"What?"

"I want you to take Wendy out of this. We've got people in Somerset."

Wendy was Bob's wife. "Take her out how?" I said.

"You can use this dinghy. I'll still have the little one."

"But this is silly, isn't it?" I said. "Why don't you take her yourself?"

"I can't, old man. I'm on duty."

Bob had always been known to his friends for what is called straight thinking; his distinctions were never blurred. He had, he reckoned, a duty to his wife to get her away from London, and his duty as a Special Constable to stay. The two would be incompatible if it were not for my help.

"We'd be stealing the dinghy though," I said.

"Can't be helped," said Bob. "Did you know the water's rising?"

"Well, of course."

"I don't just mean the rain. The level's suddenly begun to rise much faster now, but we're supposed to keep it quiet. Yesterday it was nine inches. You can't tell me that was just rainfall."

"Nine inches!"

"There's something funny going on."

I said, "There was a clergyman in the eighteenth century, who explained Noah's Flood in terms of a kind of Saturnian ring round the earth, which consisted of water, and suddenly descended. I suppose it couldn't happen twice."

"Sounds a bit far-fetched."

"Look, it is far-fetched," I said. "It could be that somebody's lit a fire under the polar ice caps. It could be that something funny has happened to the pressure at the bottom of the Atlantic. It could be that a whole new Continent has appeared, and we're getting the displaced water. Which do you prefer, Bob? You can have any of those."

"I don't know."

"Why it began isn't important. When is it going to stop?"

"Don't know that either," said Bob. "But I want Wendy out of this. It's not healthy in London." We moved on along the King's Road. "Whatever happens, she'll be better off at Chew."

Bob's parents lived on Chew Hill above the village of Chew Magna, which had at that time the smallest gasworks in England. Chew is not far from the Mendips, and part of the Government's Emergency Programme, we knew, was that temporary colonies should be set up on such areas of high ground, and there, when some sort of hutted accommodation should be ready, together with stocks of chemical foods, medicines and vitamin pills, the population should be concentrated. D-Day for the evacuation had been set for April 2nd, but it would be a process spread over some weeks. Chew Magna itself lies in a valley, but the hill rises steeply from it; Bob reckoned that his people would still be there, and within reach of the Mendip Camp when it began to function.

We tried that evening to work out a route to Chew, but we had no contour maps, and the green and brown patches of the Ordnance Survey provided only the vaguest indications. "You'll have to avoid the rivers," said Bob. "They'll be flowing against you." Even as things were, we should be unlikely to cover more than thirty miles a day.

Food would take up very little room in the dinghy. Londoners had been living on tablets—yeast tablets, dextrose tablets, vitamin tablets and large pills of various colours, labelled "Nourishment A, B, C and D" and packaged by Government laboratories. "Your Meal in a Matchbox! Science reveals that Synthetic Foods are MORE TASTY and MORE NOURISHING than food in its animal state," I had written in the early days of the shortages, and the matchbox meals were supplemented with a kind of slop, which was mostly fish and water, and was brought round daily to as many houses as could be easily reached by the

L.C.C. launches. Bob could steal enough of these tablets to last us for some time, and the slop we could make for ourselves if we caught any fish and were prepared to stomach it raw. For the rest, we would take blankets and waterproof covers, and find shelter for the nights where we could.

Rain gives insignificance to any situation. Wendy and Bob Humphries, two people of devotion and strength, parted damply from one another in the early morning. Wendy wept, but her tears went unnoticed in the rain. An improvised ladder led from the first floor of the house to the dinghy below, and half-way down she was taken by a fit of coughing, and we were afraid she would fall in the water. I followed with the bundle of blankets wrapped in water-proofing, and Bob handed down the other stores we were to take. As we pushed away from the side of the house, he leaned from the window to watch us go. "Good-bye, old girl. Keep your chin up," he said. "Take care of her, John."

I said, "I will," and pushed down hard into the water with my paddle. As we moved farther away down the street, we could see him standing there at the window, stiff and solitary. "Good-bye," I cried. Wendy had not spoken from the time we left the house, and as she lifted her hand to wave, she began to cough again.

Bob's greatest anxiety had been that he could give us no very effective weapons. Not as many people owned guns as the writers of detective stories liked to think; Bob himself, as a member of the Disposal Service, was armed, but he had only his Sten gun, and could not give that to us. What if we should be attacked? We should have to approach towns and villages along the way to get our bearings from time to time. The rubber dinghy would be a temptation to people marooned by the flood; might they not swim from their shelters and try to take it? We had a couple of kitchen knives and a bicycle chain, but Wendy, I was sure, would not be able to use either. I paddled harder for thinking of it.

I do not like to remember that time. The getting lost
—we were lost before we left the streets of London—
the days of paddling, the fishing line that trailed behind
the dinghy and never caught any fish, the damp nights
in deserted houses, and that one night we spent out in
the open, paddling on through the slanting rain, while
Wendy wept and wept as her paddle cut into the water.
He had been a boy that night (it is still confused in my
memory); he had been a boy no more than seventeen,
and when we said, "Get in then, get in," he had refused
because it was the others had sent him, and there was
no room for the others, and he had tried to pull the
dinghy back with him as he swam, and I had hit him
again and again with the paddle, and then, when he
would not let go, with the knife across the knuckles,
and he had not even cried out, but only let go, and we
did not know whether he got back to the others or not.
Only we did not stop anywhere that night, but paddled
on while Wendy wept and coughed, and coughed and
wept. Her cough grew worse through that night and all
the next day, and I knew that we should have to stop and
rest for a while.

Some way outside Faringdon we discovered another
house. A sturdy isolated building, it might have been a
vicarage, but we could see no church nearby. The ground
floor was, of course, submerged, but two other floors rose
above it, and these were furnished. In one of the cup-
boards there were sheets of old newspaper. They were
damp—the damp was almost like a mist through the
floorboards—but we managed to light them; Bob had
given us his last box of matches before we left, and we
had wrapped it like a precious thing in layers of cloth
and oilskin. We broke up chairs and made a fire, both
coughing now and red-eyed from the smoke that filled
the room.

"I expect it's a nest in the chimney," said Wendy.
Then we realized that, during the whole of our journey
so far, we had seen no birds.

After a while we grew used to the smoke—or perhaps there was less of it—and managed to dry some of the bedding we found in the house. I went out to the staircase to see whether it would be easy to break up the bannisters and treads, and so supplement our stock of wood, and I saw, floating on the surface of the water half-way up the stairs, one of the heat-resistant plastic cans in which food was preserved. It had been opened, and was empty.

"I think there's some food here if we can find the kitchen," I said.

"But it's under water."

"I'd have to dive."

Outside, grey daylight persisted; it would not be dark for several hours. But the water was dark. We looked through the hole we had made in the floorboards, and watched damp plaster fall away from the ceiling of what we had settled to be the kitchen. Floating on the surface of the water only about a foot below us was a reassuring litter of kitchen stuff—a carton of cereal, egg-shells and stray pieces of vegetable matter. "Where will the larder be?" I said.

"If you could find a cupboard."

I let myself down into the water, and swam about. It was very cold. Soon my knee hit against the top of a cupboard. I expelled the air from my lungs, and sank, groping in the dark water for the handle of the cupboard door. As I found it, and pulled, the cupboard itself leaned towards me. I felt the weight of it bearing me down, and I realized that I should die down there, ridiculously trapped beneath a kitchen cupboard on the floor, dead, drowndead, while Wendy coughed in the bedroom. I pushed violently at the cupboard, which moved a little to one side and continued to fall, and the kick of my legs carried me to the surface again.

"What happened?"

"The cupboard fell on me."

"Are you hurt?"

"No. Frightened."

It was true. I felt a very great reluctance to submerge again and try to find the cupboard on the floor. When I did so, it had fallen with the door downwards. I surfaced, and swam round the sides of the kitchen, looking for something that might be the entrance to a larder. When I found it, I was already chilled. The water reached to the larder ceiling, and I dived into a black cold box, tight-packed, it seemed, with that hostile choking water. I could see nothing. All my movements were slowed down, and when my outstretched arms touched some sort of a can, I clutched it gladly, and turned to bear it back to the surface.

I couldn't find the door; I had lost direction. The can fell out of my hand as I beat in slow motion against the larder wall. My head hit the ceiling, but there was no air there; the larder was filled with water. Something in my chest was trying to get out, trying to burst the bonds of my body, and dissipate itself in the blackness. In my fear and pain, I almost lost consciousness. I do not know how, in the end, I found the larder door and the hole in the kitchen ceiling and Wendy's hands, which reached down to help me, and to which I clung, sobbing, until I had the strength to pull myself up.

I did not dive again that day, but slept by the fire, while Wendy watched, and kept it alight. In the morning, I went back into the larder, diving again and again to bring up cans of metal polish, a rusty tin that had contained salt, pots of spoiled jam, and seventeen of the plastic cans of vegetables.

Although I don't suppose Bob Humphries had considered the possibility—or if he had done so, he must have put all his strength of will to dismissing it—the nature of our situation might have made it likely that Wendy and I should become lovers. Reading back over what I have just written, and remembering how, after she had pulled me from the water, Wendy dried me with a sheet, wrapped me in the fire-warmed smokey bedding, and lay beside me until she was sure I was tranquil again and on the way to sleep, I myself find it curious that we did not. Yet in fact the relationship that grew between us would have made sex into a kind of incest. We were too close together in the dinghy; we had no privacy, emotional or physical. And, although it was difficult and embarrassing at first to discard the habitual bodily reticences, we very soon grew used to doing so, and were as natural as children before they have been taught shame, or like Adam and Eve in the Garden before they had discovered the shattering power and pleasure their bodies could give.

We remained in the house for three days, by which time we had burned the furniture, the bannisters and stair-treads and much of the floor. Wendy's cough seemed to get no better, but we both felt rested and somehow more secure when the time came to set out again.

So we went on through that flooded countryside. The water covered the fields, and the flat bottom of the dinghy sometimes scraped the tops of hedges. We had left the Thames valley, and we were lost more frequently as we worked our way westwards along the troughs of water that lay between the hills, until every now and again the hills would come together, so that we had either to turn back or slosh through the mud and rain, dragging the dinghy to the next stretch of water.

During those days we saw neither animals nor people. Those animals which had not been drowned would long ago, we supposed, have been eaten, and the people of the villages would either be dead or have been evacuated to areas more easily supplied with food. Only once, as the grey of evening grew deeper before nightfall, we came across a little hillock surrounded by water, from which a single gaunt beast—a child's pony, by its size—stared at us. We drew nearer, and it lifted its head, and neighed, and as we paddled on into the twilight, the sound pursued us for long after the pony itself had vanished from our sight.

Eventually, still keeping out of the way of towns, we came to Somerset and to Chew Magna, and the only person alive in the flooded and deserted village below Chew Hill was a girl, floating on a piano.

3. Under Canvas

We helped the girl into the dinghy, and, with the effort, the top of the piano was pushed under water. It sank at once, and the girl began to weep.

"It's all right," said Wendy. "Don't cry. You're safe now."

"Silly old thing!" said the girl, still weeping. "I never liked it."

I said, "I think we've met before."

"Why don't you have a tuner in, I used to tell them. It's no good having a piano if it's out of tune."

"It was at a party at Bletchley. I spilled some cider cup down the front of your dress. I expect you've forgotten."

The girl stood weeping, and looked at me more closely. "It's difficult to say in that hat," she said. "Still I suppose it keeps you dry."

"You were with a ballet company. On tour."

"That's right. It was with the old Cosmopolitan before we broke up. Well, that is strange. I never did get the stains off that dress. One of the girls in Guys and Dolls when we were touring said she knew a way with salts of lemon, but we only burnt a hole in it, and I had to throw it out."

"How long had you been on that piano?"

"Hours. I got so wet, I must say. And I had to take the inside out before it would float. My name's Sonya. Sonya Banks. What's yours? By now the girl was cheerful and at ease with us, her tears forgotten. I have noticed this trait in dancers. They are astonishingly able to live in the moment, switching easily from one thought or feeling to another entirely different in subject or in kind;

32

Sonya will often do it in mid-sentence if some casual incident diverts her attention.

I introduced Wendy and myself.

"I suppose you're going to the Camp," said Sonya.

"Has it started?"

"Well, I don't know. But everybody's going to it, so I suppose it must have."

Wendy said, "My husband's parents live here. We hoped to stay with them until the Camp was ready."

"But they've all gone. They went without me."

"Who went without you?"

"Everybody. In boats and things. There wasn't anything left but the piano."

Sonya had come to stay with her aunt and uncle at Chew Magna when the company of the musical comedy in which she had been touring was disbanded after reaching Bristol. Bob Humphries, it seemed, had been mistaken in thinking that his parents would have reserves of food. The semi-rural communities were just as dependent on the deliveries of milkmen and bakers as the folk in the cities; no hams hung any longer from their ceilings. The people of Chew had been as cold and damp and hungry as the people of London; their old folk had died, and their young had sickened. While, on the one hand, they had been able to bury their dead and were free of plague, on the other they had lacked even the makeshift feeding services of the L.C.C.

Then the word had come, by air and water, from the Headquarters of Government in the West Country, that they were to prepare themselves to move to a Camp in the Mendips. That was Stage A—the Alert; detailed evacuation lists were to follow, and Stages B, C, D, E and F would see the move completed. But the people did not wait for Stages B, C, D, E and F. They moved by boat and table-top and anything that would float, and they moved at once towards the promise of food and company.

There was nobody left in the village, said Sonya, and so it proved. The long, one-storey building on Chew Hill where the Humphries had lived was as empty as any of the other deserted houses we had passed on our way. The window in Bob's old room had been left open, and the rain blew in on his boyhood books, his home-made radio set and all the healthy litter of his growing-up. The car rusted in the garage, the lawn-mower in the tool-shed; empty coops in the water-logged garden showed that there had once been chickens. In the music-room, Mrs. Humphries' grand piano stood with the top open as if for a recital; to chop it up for firing was as difficult as drowning kittens.

A picture to remember. We had found some Friars Balsam among the bathroom medicines, and we heated water to mix with it. Wendy sat inhaling, with her head over a basin, and a towel over her head, while Sonya crouched by the hearth, taking in the waist of a pair of trousers she had found among Mrs. Humphries' things. The daylight had nearly faded, and the room was lit only by the flames of the fire. Suddenly Sonya put down her work, and went over to the windows. She drew the curtains; the rain was shut out. "There," she said, smiling at us, "that's more comfortable, isn't it?" and the room and the firelight took on associations I had forgotten, and I was at home again.

In the evening of the next day, we arrived at the Mendip Camp.

I remember a sprawling area of muddy and disordered tentage, of huts half-built and over-crowded, of shelters improvised from upturned boats and furniture crowded together and draped with macintoshes. I remember the cold, and above all I remember the stench that seemed to pervade the drenched air, and every day grew stronger; it was like a concentration of all the army latrines I have ever known. There was nothing that the Camp Authorities could do about the stench; when they sent working parties out to dig new latrines, the latrines filled up with water as they were dug, and, although the people tried at first to defecate decently outside the perimeter of the camp, as it grew larger these distinctions ceased to be observed.

There was little, indeed, that the Authorities could do about anything, once the Evacuation Plan had failed. It had been intended that the first arrivals should build huts for the rest. The whole camp was to grow in prefabricated squares, stage by stage. An improvised electrical plant would provide power and warmth; the chemists had worked out some method of getting nourishment from algae artificially stimulated to rapid growth. None of this happened. The plant was never completed, and was occupied half-built by folk in search of shelter. The hut-sections, as they were dropped from the air, were parcelled out to supplement the makeshift shelters that were soon the only accommodation arrivals could get, and these were over-crowded, and when tents were set up, they were over-crowded, and the tents had floors of mud, and so did the shelters. Soft mud was everywhere. The people lived in the mud and rain like animals, and were as docile.

They were docile in their staying, docile even in their dying, but this was only, as it were, in unconscious penance for their first act of indocility, which was that they had ignored the Plan. The Mendip Camp was a trap, but a trap created by its victims; from all over the West Country, they had rushed like lemmings to their damp death. At first the Authorities had tried to turn the people away, but how could this be done?—they had no soldiers, no rolls of barbed wire, no searchlights; nobody had imagined that it would be necessary to defend the Camp. Huts were taken over for a hospital, and then more huts, and then tents, so that by the time we arrived, only the sick had accommodation that had not been improvised. The Camp Commandant, who believed that he should share the discomforts of his charges, had moved the wooden sign marked "OFFICE" from hut to tent to shelter, and, when we went to report, it was hanging crazily from one knob of a chest of drawers.

It had seemed to me that there was very little point in dragging the dinghy up-hill in the rain to the Camp. I had suggested deflating it and hiding it.

"How are we going to blow it up again?" Sonya had said.

"We shan't want to, shall we?"

"Then why are you bothering to hide it?"

"I suppose we might want it," I had said. "We'd better tie it up somewhere."

"We don't want anyone finding it and taking it for themselves. After all it is ours."

So I had hidden the dinghy in a clump of trees well above the water line. Sonya had promised she would remember the place; dancers' memories, she said, had to be better than those of other people, otherwise the classics couldn't be preserved. Our other possessions were all contained in two waterproof bundles. I had shouldered one and Sonya the other, and we had set off at a slow trudge, so that Wendy would be able to keep up.

She was by this time obviously sick. Our slow progress to the Camp had been interrupted by her spasms of coughing, during which tears flowed unrestrained from her eyes, and she kept saying, "I'm sorry to be a nuisance; I'm sorry to be a nuisance," over and over again.

"Never mind," Sonya had said. "There's bound to be a hospital when we get there. They'll soon have you right again."

But they didn't. At first Wendy refused to go into hospital at all until she had found Bob's father and mother, but we discovered that the Camp Authorities had given up trying to keep records, and that the search for Mr. and Mrs. Humphries would entail making inquiries at every shelter, so Wendy submitted, was taken to hospital, and remained there. The hospital enclosure, we found, covered an area to one side of the Camp; it was surrounded by a rough wire fence, which was continually being enlarged, as more and more tents were taken over. The hospital patients had beds of a sort; the rest of us had not. Sonya and I found quarters in a tiny improvised shelter with the frightened man. Nobody else would stay with him, but even so we had little enough room.

The frightened man sat in the mud against the piece of pre-fabricated walling that formed one side of the shelter. His hands were crossed over his chest; his knees were drawn up to his chin. We found him in this position when we arrived, and he never changed it until the day we left. The frightened man was frightened; that was all there was to him. "I am in a constant, perpetual, all-pervading state of fear," he told us. "Can you understand what that means? What you feel in occasional moments of danger, I feel all the time. I am a man stepping into an aeroplane for his first flight. I am the schoolboy who has come to the headmaster's study to be caned. I am the condemned man, waiting in his cell, facing away from the door by which the executioner will enter, waiting, waiting for the first sound that will tell him that door has opened. I am all fear, do you understand? You two, you still have your façades, making them stronger and solider and more handsomely decorated, but what lies behind the façade is what we are, and what I am is fear," said the frightened man. "My façade is broken, and I am all fear, defenceless and uncontrolled as you see me."

It was a killing time. There was so little to do. We volunteered for Camp Duties, but in that state of disorganization there were more volunteers than duties, and I found myself in a working party only once. We would join the queues for rations—the same slop (which seemed now to have grass in it) and the same tablets—and we shared our food with the frightened man, who never moved to collect any for himself. We read the notices on the Notice Board, and made little trips of exploration outside the Camp perimeter; since we were always wet, and our shelter leaked, it didn't seem to make much difference whether we were indoors or not, and we never developed a taste for the frightened man's company. And every day, for the six days and seven nights we spent at the Mendip Camp, we went to visit Wendy in hospital, standing by the side of the canvas bed on which she lay, and making such scraps of conversation as we could. Then, on the seventh morning, the hospital was out of bounds.

"What does it mean?" I said.

"What does what mean?" said the frightened man.

"The hospital. It's out of bounds."

All the short time we had known him, the frightened man had kept his eyes wide open, staring in front of him. We had never seen him close his eyes, but now he closed them. "You know what it means," he said. He put the thumb of his right hand into his mouth, rolled to one side, and lay there with his eyes tight shut. As Sonya and I left the shelter, we heard him say very distinctly, "My name was Alfred Chester. I had a practice in Chipping Sodbury".

"Can you be sure of finding the dinghy again?" I said.

Sonya said, "We can't leave Wendy."

"No."

But we couldn't reach her. They wouldn't allow it. The notice at the hospital enclosure said "Out of Bounds." When we asked at the Camp Office whether they would make an exception, and allow us to visit Wendy, they said they were sorry. "You know how it is," said the orderly. "We're not allowing any visitors now, you see. It gets so over-crowded in there."

"Yes, of course," I said.

We walked together through the rain to collect our bundles of belongings from the shelter. "Even if they did let us in," I said, "they wouldn't let us take her away. Even if they let us take her away, she wouldn't be able to travel."

Sonya said nothing.

"There isn't anything we could possibly do," I said. Sonya said nothing.

I began to talk very quickly, explaining and justifying, saying the same thing over and over again in different words. It was quite true; we could not break in, after all; we could not carry Wendy through the wire; she would

die in the dinghy, I said, knowing that she would die in
the hospital too, alone and friendless after we had gone.
I said that we had to think of ourselves, and the risk
from infection. It is not bad to be a coward; that is a
natural thing. But it is bad to make excuses and feel
ashamed. I cannot remember this occasion without shame,
but I cannot remember it without tenderness either, for
when I had finished speaking, Sonya said gently, "I know,
dear," and I realized then that I loved her, and I felt
that she loved me.

As soon as we could, we left the perimeter of the
Mendip Camp. Behind the hospital enclosure there was
a furnace, intended for baking. It had not been used,
because there was not the fuel to make its use worth-
while. But we noticed that it was in use now.

4. Interlude

The ashes of our fire still lay in the hearth at Chew Magna. We came into the house feeling like uninvited guests. Our footsteps seemed unnaturally loud on the bare boards of the music-room, now bereft of its piano.

Sonya raked out the hearth, while I chopped up a chest of drawers to make a fire. The drawers had been lined with newspaper, and the columns of print told of an old happy time before the Flood. They told of the tantrums of statesmen and Trade Union leaders and of the divorces of film stars. They told of hydrogen bomb tests, and of geneticists who protested against the increase of radioactivity in the atmosphere, and of Cabinet Ministers who accused the geneticists of communist sympathies. We read of the dangers of Britain's becoming a second-class power, of inconvenient documents suppressed, foreigners of liberal sympathies deported, private citizens dismissed from their jobs for reasons of security which they were not permitted to answer, and of Her Majesty's Home Secretary, who had remarked while opening a Charity Bazaar at Hendon, that he could not doubt that Great Britain, in these troubled times, was an example of enlightened democracy that the world would do well to copy.

We watched the flames burn away the headlines, and catch the varnish and wood of the chest of drawers. "It's a lovely fire," Sonya said. "There's no sense in sitting around in wet clothes, though. We'd better find something to change into. I'll go and look." Watching her as she left the room, watching her straight-backed graceful walk, I thought that, almost alone among artists, dancers

look like what they are. Classical dancers practise a formal
art, and wear their similarity of limb and feature like a
badge. Sonya has dark hair, parted in the middle, lying
close to her head; it is the hair you have seen so many
times, framing the too-white faces of the corps in *Les
Sylphides;* now that Sonya's hair has been often dirtied
and often washed, and unskilfully hacked about as it has
grown, it is not easy to control, but she still insists in
confining it in the same unbecoming *chignon.* Sonya's
eyes are dark, beneath eyebrows arched into a gentle V;
her legs are slim; she has neat dancer's breasts; her back
is straight. In time, she will grow old, she will bear children, and she will become (though neither of us will ever
notice it) an old dancer, bright-eyed, and dedicated, chirp-
ing her commands in bastard French to a new generation
at some improvised *barre*—even if it is no more than
she has as I write this story, a rough fence and a levelled
patch of ground, where even now she scuffs her toes in
the dusty earth.

But I did not look so far into the future at Chew; my
thoughts were not so ordered. When Sonya returned, she
was carrying a huge armful of clothing and two towels.
She threw the clothing in a pile on the floor, and handed
me one of the towels. "Let's get dried before we put our
things on," she said. "You dry me, and I'll dry you."

It was not at all as it had been with Wendy; we were
not brother and sister at all. My mouth was dry, and I
knew that my ears were red. I found that the casual
affairs of the newspaper and advertising worlds had not
prepared me for this; I was for the first time in love and
embarrassed. I turned my back on Sonya as I undressed,
tearing off my shirt and vest in one movement, but (since
my fingers shook so) taking an age to untie the laces
of my shoes.

I turned round, and Sonya was naked already. The
male body is not constituted to conceal desire. Sonya
did not pretend to be surprised; she was not off-hand
and sophisticated either; simply, she lifted her face to be

kissed. Then, after that first long searching kiss, she was very close to me, her head on my shoulder.

We sat down together awkwardly on the pile of clothing. I said, "Darling . . . darling. . . ." over and over again, and Sonya moaned a little as she closed her eyes.

After a long while she said, "I think you'd better get some wood. The fire's almost out."

5. A Life Afloat

Sonya was singing when we saw the raft. "Cruising down the river, On a Sunday afternoon, The sun above and one you love, Waiting for the moon"—however things went with us, I found, she had this simple absorption in whatever she happened to be doing at the moment. I cannot remember how many days we had spent in the dinghy now that land shelters had become dangerous. To anyone still tied to the land, we offered the possibility of escape and food, even though we had no food and no destination. My arm was gashed from one such encounter with an old wild verger, alone on a church tower.

We were, in any case, out of sight of land. We could no longer tell whether all had been submerged by the steadily rising water, or whether we had drifted into the Bristol Channel and so the sea; there seemed to be very little swell, but the water had a slightly salty taste, and we used the rain-water for drinking—"What we drink at least we don't have to bail out," Sonya had said. Both of us felt irresponsible from hunger; we had eaten nothing for some days. A man has a duty to try to live, so we bailed out the dinghy from time to time, and the useless, baitless line trailed behind us, but neither of us imagined that we should survive our voyage together.

Then we saw the raft. It was very large, and very square, and it had a sort of square outhouse set in the middle of it. There was a mast for a sail, which hung down limply, to be soaked by the thin rain. The raft rose, it seemed to us, curiously high in the water.

I said, "Shall we hail them?"

"What can we lose?"

I made a megaphone of my hands, and shouted into the rain, "Ahoy! Is anyone there?" After a moment, a door in the square outhouse opened, and a figure in yellow oilskins appeared, looked at the dinghy, and went away again.

"What's the use?" I said.

"Paddle closer."

As we drew closer to the raft, the man reappeared, accompanied by a second larger man, who was carrying what seemed to be a spear. The yellow oilskins were far too large for the smaller man, and far too yellow for anyone. "Ahoy there!" I shouted again.

"Stay where you are," said the smaller man. "If you come any closer, I shall ask Captain Hunter to jab you with his spear."

We paddled closer still, keeping just out of range. "We've warned you," the man said. "You have only yourselves to blame. Even if you were to succeed in boarding this raft, there are enough of us to do the two of you considerable harm before flinging you back in the water."

I said, "I'm sorry. We thought——"

"You'll have to answer some questions first. Who are you? Are you husband and wife?"

I said, "No," and Sonya said, "Yes."

"It doesn't matter anyway," said the man. "Circumstances have forced most of us into adopting a new view of social relationships. How old is the woman?"

"Twenty-three."

"Is she healthy?"

"I'm a bit damp," said Sonya.

"So I see. I suppose we could take the woman anyway. What do you do?"

"Do?"

"For a living."

I had a sudden moment of inspiration. "I'm a cook," I said.

"A cook!" The other man had not spoken until now.

He was a big, blond-bearded, silly-looking fellow. He grounded his spear, and looked at me hopefully. "Can you cook fish?" he said.

"I can cook anything."

The smaller man said suspiciously, "You have a very educated voice—for a cook."

"I worked for five years at the École Gastronomique in Paris." They would certainly have heard of Gaston Dufresne, who had been invented by my advertising agency to popularize a meat extract.

"I say," said the blond man. "Must be all right then."

"There is nothing to be lost by trying him," said the smaller man. "He may be able to devise a dish that incorporates your breakfast food, Captain Hunter."

"Oh, I say."

"Please allow them to board at any rate. When they have unloaded their dinghy, they may as well secure it to the raft, if there is any hook or bolt that may be adapted to the purpose."

"There's a sort of ring thing," said Hunter.

"By all means let them use the ring thing," said the smaller man.

"Why did you tell them that?" said Sonya.

"I had to tell them something."

"But why——?"

"Be quiet; they may hear you. It was obvious that they wouldn't take me on board unless I could do something useful."

"Can you cook?"

"Not very well. You'll have to help."

Sonya was silent as I completed the series of knots that secured the dinghy to Captain Hunter's ring thing. "They didn't ask me. . . ." she said slowly.

"No."

"Then?"

"No," I said. "Don't worry. We'll think of something.

We'll stay together. I'll be near you all the time. It'll be all right."

But when we came to climb on to the raft from the dinghy, which lay lower in the water, we found that we had even less strength than we had thought, and I could not believe that, if the need came, I should make a very effective bodyguard.

The smaller man was Arthur Renshaw. He was an accountant. Someone (I think it was P. G. Wodehouse) once wrote of a character, "Behind his spectacles, his eyes gleamed with the light of pure intelligence". Arthur was like that—absurd and frightening. He had thin lips, and a thin face, and thin hair, lying flat against his head. He had high cheek-bones, and hair grew on them. He was in practical command of the raft, although his arrival on board had been as fortuitous as our own.

The raft belonged to the International Unitarian Breakfast Food Company. It was made of balsa wood, and liberally stocked with Glub, the Ideal Breakfast Food: You Need No Other. It had been the contention of the International Unitarian Breakfast Food Company that man could live by Glub alone. As the Atlantic and Pacific Oceans began to fill up between 1955 and 1960 with balsa-wood rafts, criss-crossing in contrary directions to reach different anthropological and oceanographical conclusions, the Company had outfitted a raft of its own, and commissioned Captain Hunter to command it. He was to sail around the world on it; Glub was to be his food, and distilled sea-water his drink. Glub contains every known vitamin, as well as protein, carbo-hydrates and all the elements needed to sustain life. Glub comes in any shape—Glub Grits, Glub Cushions, Glub Toasties, Glub Flakes, Poppity Glub for the Little Ones, Glub Mash, and of course the new Glub in a Matchbox—A Week's Nourishment in Your Pants' Pocket. Glub is protein and has many uses; it can be eaten for breakfast with hot or cold milk or with fruit, for lunch with cheese or for dinner with meat, or even instead of meat (Glub

Cutlets for vegetarians); moistened and moulded, Hunter had discovered, it is an excellent bait for fish if the fish are hungry.

I remembered the photographs and publicity when Hunter set off. But there was so much of that sort of thing then; it sometimes seemed that hardly a day passed without a group of students setting out for Australia in a ketch. It had all been some time ago, and quickly forgotten; it had occurred to nobody to find out how Hunter was getting on. After all, the voyage was bound to take some time; it had taken Sir Francis Drake three years in a much faster vessel.

Hunter had drifted with many currents, sailed before many winds. His distaste for Glub had made of him a skilful fisherman with spear and line. Landing once on an uninhabited island, he had discovered the joy of coconuts and goats which ran wild, but his sense of duty to his employers drove him on: "Besides," he said, "I was due the whale of a lot of back pay." He got lost. He had never been much good at navigation ("used to leave that kind of thing to the N.C.O.'s") and by the end of the first year he had ceased to have much idea where he was, since in any case there was so little he could do about controlling the direction in which his craft travelled—you can run before the wind in a raft after you have used your rudder to manœuvre you into the right position, but you cannot sail into it. At some time during his voyage, the rain had begun, and had not stopped, but it had not occurred to him to think this odd.

I once asked him how he had come to apply for the job.

"Read a book about it," he said, "I mean, I had to do something. I tried out for keeping a pub, as a matter of fact, but they wouldn't have me. Something to do with I.Q.: you had to do mental arithmetic, and underline words and all that stuff. Then a pal of mine told me about this job; said they were looking for an open-air type. I must say it sounded very jolly. You know—shirt-off stuff and all that."

He was a shirt-off kind of man, never so happy as when he was stripped to the waist and growing a beard. He should have stayed in the army, but they got, he said, so bloody technical. Besides, he had no real talent for command, not even for the pretence of it; his N.C.O.'s must have bullied him atrociously. On the other hand, he was very good at taking orders. He would certainly have jabbed away at us with that spear if Arthur had told him to do so, although he was not an unkind man, and I never saw him lose his temper.

Muriel and Wesley Otterdale were the next we met of the raft's complement. We found them in the galley, where Muriel was trying to make a stew of fish-heads.

The galley was only one room of the four which made up the living quarters of the raft. They had been fitted up by the International Unitarian Breakfast Food Company like a bachelor flat in Knightsbridge; there was a living-room, a bedroom, a kitchen and a bathroom (with salt-water shower). The lights and the stove were worked by electricity, which was made on board the raft itself. Small wheels of some very light metal (was it lithium, or is that one of the metals which explodes in water?) were mounted just below the waterline. Each was curiously indented with cup-shaped veins, and as the raft moved in the water, these wheels revolved, charging the storage batteries by which the raft was powered. Their capacity was enormous; although the raft had been frequently becalmed during the last few months by the heavy rain, the supply of electrical power had been easily maintained.

All the floor of the raft was hollow, and formed an immense hold. In it were barrels and crates of Glub in its various forms, a spare sail, tools—all that. Hunter must have lived very comfortably when he was on the raft alone, and even as things were, we found ourselves inconceivably better off than we had been in the Camp. The men slept in the living-room, the women in the bedroom, Muriel

Otterdale told us. Fishing and cooking duties had been organized on a roster, and those people not so engaged were put by Arthur to some useful task. There were always things to be done.

"What sort of things?" I said.

"Making nets. Stuffing the cracks in the barrels with string."

"Caulking," said Wesley. It was the first time he had spoken. "It makes the toilet smell of glue."

"You mustn't be despondent, dear."

"Don't go on at me, Muriel," said Wesley. "I get enough of that from the parson."

"I'm sorry, dear."

"What parson?" I said.

"Mr. Banner. He's always telling my husband not to worry about things."

"He makes me tired," said Wesley.

Sonya said, "I don't see why you shouldn't worry if you want to."

"No more do I," said Wesley. "No more do I. When a man's soul is troubled like mine is, I don't see why he shouldn't worry a little. Worry!—" he took the wooden spoon from the stew he was stirring, and gazed at us; his eyes were large and sad, and the line of his moustache looked unnaturally black against the pallor of his face. "I can't sleep. I lie awake there, worrying and worrying."

"I wish you could do something about it," Muriel said, "speak to Arthur or something. We're not used to sleeping apart, you see; we never have, right from the first, never twin beds or anything like that. Being married yourselves, you'd understand. We wouldn't mind sleeping in the kitchen, if we could be together. But Arthur won't see it like that. He's so orderly."

"What do you worry about, Mr. Otterdale?" I said.

"Guilt."

"It's all nonsense," Muriel said, "Mr. Banner keeps telling him, but he won't take any notice. It wasn't his fault anyway, even if God was likely to be so vindictive."

"Guilt!" said Wesley again. "Guilt and silliness! The Lord thy God is a jealous God. He will not suffer guilt and silliness to go unpunished."

"It was the police wouldn't believe him, and quite right too."

I said, "But what did you do?"

"I murdered my wife's mother."

"Goodness!" said Sonya. "Why didn't they hang you for it?"

"They wouldn't. The fools! I told them and told them, and they did nothing about it whatever. Would you believe," he said, "I asked to be punished. God knows I was willing."

"It's all nonsense really," said Muriel confidentially. "He never even hit her."

"I killed the old woman as surely as if I had cut her into little pieces before your eyes. I'm guilty, and I should be punished; that's all there is to it."

It was a silly story. Muriel's mother had lived with them ever since they had married. She seems to have been a particularly malicious old lady, and she had never approved of Wesley. For so long he had put up with her little bits of spite and her nagging and her constant presence by the family fireside, but the breaking point had come one Christmas Day when she had topped all spite by telling him to his face that he was impotent. It was something to do with his getting her the wrong Christmas present: "You've never been able to give me anything I wanted," she had said, "not even a grandson."

There had been no question of putting her away in an Old Folks' Home; she wouldn't have agreed to go. So Wesley had decided to kill her. He had cherished the idea, rolling it about in his mind for months, but when that pleasure grew stale he went about the job methodically enough. He made his will, caught up on his work at the office, and, choosing a night when Muriel was out at the Women's Institute, took the kitchen cleaver upstairs to the bathroom, where his mother-in-law was washing out a pair of stockings.

Sonya said, "But how could you get away with it?"

"I didn't want to," said Wesley, "I'd have hanged for Mother and welcome, but they wouldn't have me."

"Why not?"

"Because he didn't do it," said Muriel, "that's why not."

"I did. In all but the act, I did. Mother looked up at me from the wash-basin. 'Put that thing down at once, Wesley,' she said. And when I saw her looking at me so straight and vindictive, I put the cleaver down on the toilet seat, you see, and started to cry."

"Then?"

"It was the concentration of it, I suppose; she was always telling us she wasn't strong. She stood there with the wet stockings in her hand. 'I'll not forget this, Wesley,' she said. Then she caved in at the knees, and fell on the floor. I lifted her up, and slopped some water over her, and carried her back to her room, but it was too late. She never spoke again before she died. I killed that old woman."

"No such thing."

"I killed her. Muriel didn't want me to, but I went to the police, and spoke out what I knew. But they wouldn't take any notice. I murdered her, and I ought to suffer for it. You can't tell me God isn't punishing the world, when such evil is allowed to flourish."

"Well!" said Sonya.

Wesley said, "We are all guilty. I am guilty because I killed my wife's mother, and you are guilty because you allow me to do it. You don't think I ought to be punished, I know that."

"Well, no, I don't," I said, "I think you've probably punished yourself too much already."

"You're right there," said Muriel.

"Fools!" Wesley said, "The earth is given over to a kingdom of fools, and the Lord is wrath. He sendeth the waters from on high, and those who have turned away from righteousness shall be swallowed up."

"I never heard such nonsense," said Sonya.

"That's just what Mr. Banner told him. Mr. Banner being a clergyman, you'd think Wesley would listen. Miracles, he said; there's no such thing as miracles nowadays, he said; the Church doesn't take any account of Divine Punishment. He sat there on the roof of our house with Wesley for hours and hours, explaining to him how that Flood in the Bible had really been caused by the earth shifting its axis or something, and how God was just a spirit inside us, but it didn't do any good. Once Wesley has an idea inside that head of his, he won't change it," Muriel said tearfully, "I know. It was just the same over Mother."

Another picture stays in my mind.

We had unloaded the dinghy and put it away in the hold, when we saw Tony Ryle, the body-builder.

Tony Ryle was fishing. At one edge of the raft, by the lashed steering bar, there was a little shelter like a sentry-box, and in this he sat. From the back you could see only the wet wooden shelter, peaked at the top, the smooth sea beyond, and the rain like a thickness in the air. From the side, the rod and line projected from the box-like decoration, and so did Tony's head, wet with the rain as he watched the float.

Just as, Aristotle tells us, every man has within him the possibility of the Good Man, so Tony's shape was raw material for the Good Shape, and he had gone a long way towards achieving it. Broad of shoulder, narrow of waist, thick of neck, curly of hair, Tony sat, like God, brooding over the face of the waters in the rain and the evening twilight.

"You'll be wanting to shave," said Arthur.

"Oh, I don't know."

"You'll find a razor in the bathroom. There's no hot

water—we try to conserve power to that extent—but the rain water is very soft."

"But I don't want to."

"We like to keep ourselves looking neat. I have always found that a man who allows his appearance to go to pieces, goes to pieces mentally and morally as well."

"What about soap?"

"You will have to manage without. The skin soon gets used to it."

Banner's face, Wesley's, Tony's, Arthur's own face; all bore the scars of cold water, soapless shaving. "Captain Hunter has a beard," I said.

"He had it when we came."

Hunter said, "I keep it trimmed, you know."

"Will you say grace please, Mr. Banner?" said Arthur.

"For what we have just received, may the Lord make us truly thankful."

"Amen." Sonya grinned at me across the table; she and I had been the only two people at supper who had been able to finish our portions of fish-head stew.

"We don't allow irreverence here," said Arthur. "Not for any superstitious reasons—I am an agnostic myself—but because we find that an element of formality at meal-times helps to remind us that we are civilized beings."

Mr. Banner said, "We're all agnostics nowadays. In a manner of speaking."

"I'm not," said Sonya, and Muriel, emboldened, added, "Nor am I, I'm sure."

"That will do," Arthur said. "You'll find the razor on the top shelf of the bathroom cabinet, Mr. Clarke. Please clean it after use."

I was not in the mood or position to dispute Arthur's leadership. Indeed, Sonya and I were simply grateful for the tidy behaviour that was expected of the raft-dwellers; whatever "new view of social relationships" Arthur had adopted did not seem to include rape. I left the table obediently, and went into the bathroom.

Arthur followed me. "I wanted a word with you, Mr.

Clarke," he said. "As a new arrival, you are not yet used to our ways here, and, if you wish to stay, I am afraid you will have to adapt yourself to them."

"Of course," I said.

"I don't know whether you have come to any explanation in your mind about this Flood?"

"God?"

Arthur smiled tolerantly. "So Mr. Otterdale would tell you," he said, "and Mr. Banner would say the whole thing is due to a fine dust of silver oxide, which has somehow penetrated the earth's atmosphere from outer space. As an agnostic, I am not interested in supernatural explanations, Mr. Clarke. But one thing is certain. Whether the Flood is intended as a Divine Punishment or not, it is the best thing that could ever have happened."

"What?"

"I do a lot of reading in my spare time," said Arthur. "I have never believed that time should be squandered; a man who is not interested in improving himself is not worth the gift of reason, in my view."

"I gather who-is-it—Tony?—agrees with you."

"Mr. Ryle, he tells me, is a body-builder; that is to say, he is a narcissist of a rather stupid kind. He is not interested in mental discipline, Mr. Clarke. I myself, on the other hand, have been practising the strictest mental disciplines ever since I was a boy. I do a great deal of reading. If I had not done so, I should not be in command here."

"No."

"And if I were not in command, it is doubtful whether any of you would survive."

"You think we shall then?"

"Of course. Why else have I already set the crew to work making nets, caulking water barrels, improvising rough furniture from the empty crates in the hold? All these things will be useful to us when we land. I have it all arranged, Mr. Clarke. Natural Selection is responsible for the Flood, and by Natural Selection certain people will survive it. I shall be one of them, and so, if you are careful to follow my orders, will you."

"And all of us here?"

"Naturally."

"Just why, do you think, did Natural Selection——?"

"I can see that you are not a serious student of human affairs, Mr. Clarke."

"So much of my life has been spent in the kitchen," I said.

"Perhaps. Then let me use a kitchen metaphor to explain matters to you. Have you noticed what happens when you have too much of any foodstuff, Mr. Clarke?—too much meat? too many loaves of bread? too many bottles of milk? too many tomatoes? They go bad, and spoil. That is what has happened to the human race. Recently there have been too many people in the world, and they have been increasing at an increasing rate. Did you know, for instance, that the population of Ceylon was increasing at a rate of about 3 per cent a year—by three out of every hundred in the first year, 3.09 out of every hundred the next—the whole process had an accelerator built in. In three generations or so, we should have used up the natural resources of the earth, and reverted to a state of the most appalling barbarism. I tell you, Mr. Clarke, if it had not been for this Flood, there would have been disaster before very long."

"You mean we've been saved from race-suicide by an act of—well, Nature if you like?" I said.

"Nothing of the kind. If you wish to understand what I am saying, you will do better not to interrupt. Not only were men increasing their numbers at a terrifying rate, but the poorer, more brutish sort were increasing at a rate faster than the others. Have you any idea of the rate of mental deficiency in Great Britain over the past fifty years? No, of course you haven't. The proportion of morons and near-morons has increased because, although one can persuade intelligent people to practise birth control, one cannot teach contraceptive methods to idiots, and large families have persisted among people of low intelligence. In other words, men have increased their numbers while lowering their quality; idiots have increasingly outnumbered the intelligent, and, under a system of democracy, had as much political power." He took off his spectacles to polish them, and I noticed that his hands were trembling. "Lunacy!" he said. "It was lunacy."

"I see."

"The Flood has wiped all that out. Only intelligent people will survive it, and such of the stupid people as they choose to carry with them."

"Why carry any?"

"For the rough work. You observed Mr. Ryle's physical proportions. He will be very useful to us when the waters subside, and we begin our settlement. And with careful cross-breeding——"

"What if they never subside at all?"

"Of course they will subside," Arthur said angrily. "Of course they will. Do you imagine Natural Selection intends to replace us by fish?"

In fact, I did find a way to use Glub in the cooking; it turned out that I was a good cook of the sort which improves by experimenting. Glub Grits pounded together made a substitute for breadcrumbs, and I invented a kind of oil by crushing the scales and viscera of fish. The day we had fried fillets of cod, my claim to be a graduate of the Ecole Gastronomique was recognized.

I have said something already of Arthur and Hunter, something of the Otterdales. The others of our party were Harold Banner, Tony Ryle and Gertrude Harrison, who used to teach Voice and Dramatic Art to private pupils in an Earl's Court mews flat.

Banner, the clergyman, had been rescued with the Otterdales. He had become their lodger in the early days of the Flood when his own rectory, a Nissen hut in the churchyard, had become uninhabitable, and he had remained with them. I understood that they had spent several days together in a rowing boat. Wesley would not row, because to save himself would have been contrary to God's will, and Banner had not allowed Muriel to do so. His hands were raw when the raft picked them up, and still bore the scars. He told me that, during his university days when he went in for this kind of thing, the blisters had always turned into calluses eventually, and he had supposed they would do so again.

Tony Ryle did not tell me much about himself at that time. I gathered that he had worked for a printing firm as a machine-minder. He had always been interested, he said, in improving his physique. To "improve one's physique" —and not to body-build—is, I discovered, one of the body-builders' stock phrases. The key word is "proportion"; if you don't improve your physique proportionately, you might as well not improve it at all. In fact Tony had concentrated the area of his improvement on the chest, back and shoulders, and, although his legs were sturdy and well-shaped enough, one felt that their only purpose was to support the massive and knotted triangle of his trunk.

Most human beings want to be admired. Some men can sing, play the piano in pubs, add up columns of figures in record time, write plays or sonatas, paint, grow giant vegetable marrows; but all these activities demand, not only application, but some sort of inborn talent. Body-building requires only a body, and the slighter it is to begin with, the better: "I was a Seven-Stone Weakling" is the beginning of the body-builders' Cinderella story. Tony had never been a seven-stone weakling, but he had thought people laughed at him when he went bathing at the local open-air pool; "I never had no chest," he said, "I was sort of puny really." He was not sort of puny any more. Even on the raft he had made himself some weights and a piece of board, and he used to go down to the hold every day to practise. When Sonya found this out, she insisted on practising too, and Arthur encouraged them; he was very much in favour of recreational activities, and said that men had been kept alive in lifeboats by playing guessing games. The two of them would stand there, a little unsteadily as the raft tilted from side to side in the gentle swell, and Tony would lift his weights while Sonya did a simple *barre*, using two crates piled one on top of the other.

Tony never talked much. He would do his exercises, or fish, or scrub out the galley, or perform any of the other jobs Arthur would think up for us, his blue eyes always a little anxious, as if each activity took up the whole of his attention and left none over for conversation. If one of us were to appeal to him in discussion he would say, "Well, I don't know really," and the discussion would roll past him while he was still sorting out his ideas. (In this he did not resemble Hunter, who regarded ideas of any sort as not concerning him.) Only Sonya would have the patience to wait for Tony. "He's a nice boy," she would say, "and I don't think they ought to go so fast."

Fastest of all was Gertrude. She had no patience in talking. All conversations were to her vehicles for emotion: "There is so much to give," she would say. "One must give it all." All her life, Gertrude had been giving. She had given to her friends, her pupils and (less frequently as time went by) to the Public, and the more she had given, the more she had to give; the process was self-renewing.

Gertrude gushed. It was not the gushing of a silly ill-informed woman, but the gushing of an oil-well—all good rich stuff, and from the heart. I am sure she must have been an excellent teacher because she had no sense of the ridiculous; you could make a fool of yourself with her, and if only you *felt* what you were doing, Gertrude would not see the foolishness, and neither would you. I can remember her standing on the table in the cabin after supper, delivering Mark Antony's oration to the citizens, her arms two flexible pistons of indignation, her breasts quivering, breaking off from time to time to explain the psychological implications of the situation; and somehow what should have been supremely silly became a moving theatrical experience.

None of this did for Tony. He could not understand it, and she would not stop for him; her pupils, I suppose, had taken what they could use from the generous flood, and if they took only a twentieth of what there was, it was still enough. And, surprisingly in such a woman, she was impatient with him. Naturally sympathetic to atmosphere as any actress must be, she had caught from Arthur a little of the scorn he felt for Tony, and it remained at the back of her mind as a feeling that Tony was not "one of our kind of people". And so, although she appealed to him sometimes (she appealed to everyone; she would have appealed to the gulls of the air to confirm a point of feeling), she did not wait for him, or notice his bewilderment and pain when he was snubbed.

What surprised me was that she should think highly of Arthur; surely he was not "one of our kind of people"? She had so little in common with him, except to complement his narrowness with her breadth, his bile with her richness. What circumstances had first brought them together, I could not discover; Gertrude who would talk freely of her life in the old days, was reticent about her escape from London. Arthur had met her, and had picked her up, and had taken her with him until they found safety together on the raft. She seemed to admire him and to accept his leadership completely; I had not the courage to ask her whether she actually liked Arthur, nor am I certain whether she knew.

Arthur was holding an after-supper conference. "We shall have to think about scurvy," he said.

"We shall have to think about mould," said Sonya, "I'm sure the Glub'll have penicillin growing all over it if this goes on much longer."

"It's vacuum packed," said Hunter.

Muriel said, "We shall have to think about rheumatism. It can't be healthy, never having dry underwear."

"I have already thought of that. We shall light the stove one day a week."

"Oh bliss!"

"What shall we use for fuel?" I said.

"Driftwood."

"But it's wet."

"We shall use some of the wooden crates in the hold to start the fire. Driftwood will be stacked close to the stove to dry, ready for use on the next occasion when further driftwood will be similarly dried. Is that clear?"

"Dear Arthur!" said Gertrude. "At all times so far-seeing!"

I said, "But if we do that, can't we keep the fire going all the time? There's plenty of driftwood."

There was a moment of silence. Arthur's mouth contracted, and his adam's apple jerked a little. "There is no reason why not," he said, "provided that somebody is always on hand to keep the stove from going out."

Ridiculously I found myself a little frightened. Arthur, so benign a leader at other times in his acid way, lost all his benignity if one suggested altering any detail of his plans; I should have phrased my suggestion more tactfully. But, while hostility from Arthur might have been expected, there was more than that. In that moment of silence I could feel the hostility spreading from Arthur to Gertrude, to Hunter, to the Otterdales, to Banner. I could hear the sound of the rain and the tick of the electric clock. Sonya moved from her place by the empty stove, and came and stood by my side. "Of course," I said, "it might be difficult to find enough driftwood. I'm sure you're right, Arthur. I'm sorry."

"Perhaps we shall be able to light the stove more frequently later on when we see how easily the wood is collected," said Arthur. "I had been thinking of something of that sort. Meanwhile let us return to the problem of scurvy."

Drinking water was kept in a two-gallon bottle in the cabin. Whenever a new lot had been distilled, the contents of a small phial of lemon juice concentrate was added to it, so that our drinking water always tasted a little of fresh lemonade. Hunter had disclosed, however, that the supply of this concentrate was almost exhausted. "There is no doubt," Arthur said, "that our diet is in danger of vitamin deficiency."

"My fault really," Hunter said, "I thought we might as well use the stuff while we had it. Never thought it mattered about— Well, I mean, isn't Glub supposed to take care of that kind of thing? It says on the packet——"

"No."

"Does it have to be lemons?" Sonya said. "Or would any sort of green stuff do?"

"I suppose it would."

"Seaweed?"

Arthur considered, "There are edible seaweeds," he said, "just as there are edible fungi. I should not undertake, however, without some sort of expert. . . ."

Sonya said, "There was some stuff called dulse. They used to sell it in paper bags. Sort of chewy only rather salt. It was like dried red cabbage."

Gertrude said, "I'm sure the texture would be almost Chinese. I adore Chinese food. If you would like a guinea pig——"

"No, let me," said Mr. Banner. "One need not take very much, after all, to try it. I remember that we conducted an experiment into the effects of mescalin at the Townswomen's Guild. I was the guinea pig for that also, and really, you know, it was not at all unpleasant; rather as if one were seeing one's body for the first time. I felt as if I had been dipped in concrete, I remember, which had hardened on me, but beneath the brittleness of my skin, there was a quite extraordinary amount of life in——"

"Perhaps Mr. Clarke would care to taste the seaweed," Arthur said. "He would in any case have to do so in the cooking."

"By all means. You'd like it served as a vegetable, I imagine."

"I'm sorry, darling."

"Sorry, Miss Banks?"

"I mean, I'm sorry it was my suggestion that— Wouldn't it be fairer if we——?"

"But it was a very sensible suggestion," said Arthur. "I am sure we shall all benefit from it."

In a sense, we did. All the seaweed I tasted was rubbery and quite inedible, but we added the water in which it was boiled to our meals of fish, and had our vitamins that way, I suppose.

Cooking, cleaning, fishing, so the time passed. Collecting driftwood, exercising in the hold, mending our clothes, so the time passed. Listening to the rain and wondering when it would stop, the time passed; holding evening entertainments and discussions on uncontroversial subjects, the time passed; watching the progress of foot-rot between the toes, the time passed; lying apart, segregated by sexes in cabin and bedroom, the time passed. Making do, the time passed; socks were darned with the unravelled sacking, toothbrushes improvised from the shredded twigs of a branch that floated by. Captain Hunter taught Banner to play the schoolboys' game of book-cricket by opening at random the pages of the Bible or the Oxford Illustrated Dictionary, and in the evenings Gertrude read aloud to us from the Old Testament—the greatest dramatic narrative of them all, she said. All the books on board, Oliver Twist, The Rubayat of Omar Khyam, Breakfast Cereals: 1952, The Collected Plays of William Shakespeare, Better Sight Without Glasses, A Hundred Best Novels Condensed, Rogue Herries, Jamaica Inn, Making and Doing in the House, Making and Doing in the Garden, Britain's Beauty Spots, several books by Peter Cheyney and a number of navigational and technical works, all were read many times.

How many days did we continue like this? It cannot have been so long a time, but it soon seemed as if it had been for ever, and would be. We grew into a routine. My temper does not accept authority easily, but I accustomed myself to Arthur's leadership, nor did Sonya question it, since the details of who did what in our everyday adminis-

tration were not important to her. It was, after all, easier
to do what we were told, and wise to submit to a discipline
if we were not to fret one another to pieces. So we grew
accustomed to the life and to each other, and time passed.

Our complement was not increased. We cannot have
been far from land, for we found flotsam in plenty—
wood, occasional movables, a few dead bodies, from which,
when we could get close enough to them, Arthur insisted
we should strip the clothing (but usually it was perished,
and the bodies gnawed by fish). We salvaged a deserted
rowing boat, and towed it behind us; it had to be bailed
out every eight hours, which made another task for Arthur
to allot on his daily list. We saw no other vessels at this
time. The steadily falling rain confined our field of vision,
and our small world was empty. I asked Arthur what he
would do if we came across any other survivors, and he
replied that it would depend; he did not think anyone we
found now would be in a condition to "pull his weight in
the boat".

Once at night some of us thought we heard a faint call
in the darkness. Arthur said it was nothing, but he allowed
us to go on deck and look. Faintly in the night and rain,
some of us thought we saw a yellow light not far away,
but Arthur said it was probably phosphorescence; what
light, in any case, could keep alive in the wet? We went
inside again.

We worked on at caulking barrels, at contriving rough
furniture from salvaged driftwood—Gertrude even tried to
make a waterproof cloak from woven seaweed, but it was
not a success. All this, Arthur told us, was against our future life when the waters would subside again, but I do
not think we took any great thought for that time; we just
did what we were told.

We were surprisingly healthy. As the routine of regular
meals, clothes that could now be dried and the more and
more frequent warmth of the stove took charge of us,
we grew stronger; even my foot-rot was checked. Bounded
by the four sides of the raft, secure within its cabin from

the rain, we felt life take on a kind of normality again. Only Wesley Otterdale did not lose his haunted hollow look, and Muriel, lying apart from him at night with the rest of the women, worried and pined for him.

Then the tempest came.

6. The Tempest

The raft had been provided with a set of diaries in octavo, a page to a day; the intention had been that Hunter should keep a log. Most of the pages in the earlier volumes were blank, the occasional entries brief: "Thunder today", or "Trouble with sharks". Since Arthur had taken over, these entries had become much more detailed, the log was written up every evening after supper. And the rest of us, although we had lost the sense of time and date before, could now tell Tuesday from Thursday again, and twelve from two.

It was on the morning of the 26th of June 1966, that the tempest struck. I was fishing. Something had made me remember the season. I sat in the little shelter from which we fished, and remembered June.

I remembered rainy Junes and sunny Junes. I remembered Sundays by the Serpentine, with the gramophones' discordances, and the Teddy Boys snatching self-consciously at each others' towels. I remembered country cricket matches and river bathing, and punting down the green corridor of the Cherwell from Magdalen Bridge on drowsy afternoons. All those Oxford Junes! I remembered commemoration balls and college gardens, making notes in the sunny spaciousness of the Codrington Library, terrible parties with cucumber cup in the garden of the Perch Inn, and one curiously final morning on which I walked round Radcliffe Square over and over again in the sunlight, sucking at peppermints and waiting for my Viva. Then there was that neurotic summer session at the University of Indiana, when I washed cutlery in the canteen of a campus dormitory and wrote papers on the criticism of Eliot and Matthew Arnold. I remembered Junes by the sea—the dreary pier at Bournemouth, the aquarium at Blackpool, beach after beach littered with ice-cream papers, and the English making holiday glumly together in cotton dresses and cloth caps, sitting bolt upright in deck chairs or against the wall of the promenade. I remembered a writing holiday in a stone cottage not far from Blaenau Festiniog, where we had to empty our nightsoil secretly into a mountain stream. I remembered willow trees and midges and mosquitoes, and the Indian June of the monsoon season, though even the monsoon rains, I remembered, were intermittent and heavier when they came than this persistent and for-ever downpour. *June is bustin' out all over*, I thought; but not this June, not this rainy June, which had followed a rainy May and would give place to a rainy July, a rainy August, month after rainy month, and year by year, while the waters rose, and our children were born with scales and a tail.

Rain, rain, go away. Come again another day, I said aloud, for the rain was blowing on my face, not falling in a straight line as it usually did. *It's raining; it's pouring. The old man is snoring. He went to bed, and he bumped his head, and he couldn't get up in the morning.* The rain was blowing on my face, not steadily but as if somebody high in the sky where the rain curtain began were shaking it lazily, so that the curtain undulated. And the swell below the raft, I noticed, was much more pronounced.

I wound in my fishing line, and went into the cabin. "There's a wind getting up or something," I said. Arthur was making up a list. He put his ball-point pen down on the table, and looked up. The table tilted, and the pen rolled off on to the floor. Arthur rose, and began to don his absurd yellow oilskins.

"I doubt if there's anything we can do about it," I said.

"We can at all events see what is happening."

The two of us went on deck together. The swell was stronger now, and, as we looked towards the east, we seemed to be looking up an incline. There was a rail running round the outside of the cabin wall, and Arthur told me to keep hold of it. The wind was still blowing fitfully, but without much power.

Towards the east, the universal grey of the sky seemed to have become several shades darker. "Captain Hunter," Arthur called. "Would you come out here, please?"

Hunter appeared at the cabin door, the others crowding behind him. "What's happening?" Sonya said.

I said, "I'd stay inside if I were you."

Arthur said, "A sensible suggestion. It would be better if all the women were to remain inside the cabin. Mr. Banner, perhaps you will see to that. Captain Hunter and Mr. Otterdale will stay here with us."

The raft, which had been tilting for a long time in one direction, suddenly went over the crest of what had ceased to be swell and was definitely a wave. The women, Tony and Mr. Banner fell backwards into the cabin, and the door slammed shut. Hunter said, "It looks as if we're in for a bit of a blow." Then a smaller wave reared suddenly up, and smacked the raft sideways; I felt like a flea on an ice-hockey puck. The top of the wave broke over the deck, and soaked us. Arthur gasped for breath, and said, "Captain Hunter, what action do you usually take under these circumstances?"

Hunter said, "I take down the sail. Then I go inside and shut the door. There's a sort of shutter thing you pull across to keep the water out. Gets a bit stuffy after a while. The fishing hut comes to bits, and you stow it inside. Doesn't take a moment. We'll do the sail now, if you like."

In the fitful wind, we negotiated the damp canvas of the sail.

"What about the rowing boat?" I said.

"I suppose we'll have to junk it."

"We shall do no such thing," said Arthur. "We must take it inside with us. We shall need the wood, even if we do not use it as a boat. If Captain Hunter will dismantle the hut, the three of us will get the rowing boat indoors."

"My God! Look at that," said Hunter, and pointed out to sea.

Through the rain we saw that the darkness in the eastern sky had drawn closer to us. We saw that it was not darkness at all, but a wave, an enormous wave, rushing upon us. There was no time to do anything but grasp the rail, as the raft tilted to a sixty-degree angle and, as it seemed, ran or was drawn to the top of the wave, danced for a moment crazily on the crest, and almost capsized as it began to fall down the further slope. Now the wind hit us with appalling force. The little fishing hut was lifted into the air, and sailed away, light and independent, back over the top of the wave again. The rain was driven into our faces like hail, and I cried aloud with the pain, and closed my eyes. As I opened my mouth to shout, the wind filled it, and I might have popped like a paper bag if we had not at that moment dropped deep enough into the trough between our first wave and the next to be sheltered once more from the wind and even from the rain, which was now passing overhead.

"Got to get inside," said Hunter.

"Save the boat."

"How?"

"Rope," said Arthur. "Rope."

Wesley said, "The Lord is mighty in anger. He sendeth the storm to chastise us."

"I dare say."

Arthur opened the cabin door, and jumped inside as the raft began its journey up towards the crest of the second wave. There was no time for us to follow him. Wesley had let go the rail, but I caught him by the collar of his jacket and held him fast, turning my face to the wall of the cabin and lowering my head as far as I could into my chest as a shelter against the wind and rain. Up we went and up. In the moment before the wind struck, I heard Wesley begin to pray aloud.

That moment came, and almost drained me of terror as the raft was juggled by the crest of the wave, and I did not know whether it would fall forwards to be overwhelmed or capsize backwards down the almost oblique outer slope. Once again, I felt the full force of the wind, and the rain like gravel against my body. I held the rail with one hand, Wesley's jacket with the other. There was a violent wrench. Then I had both hands round the rail again, and then the calm came again, and Arthur reappeared with a cut on his forehead and the rope tied round his waist.

"Where is Mr. Otterdale?" he said.

"I was holding him," I said.

Hunter said, "You aren't now."

"I know. He was praying."

Arthur said, "Help me with this rope".

"I must have let him go," I said.

"We should just have time to fix it."

Arthur threaded the other end of the rope over the rail, and then tied it around Hunter's waist. There was a great deal of slack in between. "You must let us out gradually, Mr. Clarke," he said. Then, as we survived the third wave, conversation ceased.

The rowing boat was tied up to one end of the raft, but the second wave had lifted it and flung it, with some damage to the timbers, on to the deck of the raft itself. Somehow, heavy and cumbersome as it was, it would have to be unlashed and pulled inside the cabin while we were momentarily becalmed between one giant wave and the next. Arthur and Hunter scampered out to the edge of the deck, and I took in the slack of the rope around my own body. They had succeeded in unlashing the boat, when the raft tilted as we were again drawn up the slope of a wave. The boat began to slide along the deck towards the cabin wall. I saw it coming, and moved quickly to one side; this sudden movement of mine, combined with the tilting of the deck, jerked Arthur and Hunter off their feet, so that they rolled over each other, and finished in a heap against the wall.

We reached the top of the wave. Once again the curling tip flicked the raft into the air. The rowing boat was jerked up, fell—mercifully away from us—against the cabin wall, and was lost overboard. Arthur and Hunter were tossed along the deck the length of the rope, like bait on an angler's line, and fell back again. Arthur, who was underneath, took the full force of this, and as one knee crashed against the cabin wall, he gave a shrill cry. As we dropped again into the trough, I took in the slack, and Hunter managed to get to his feet, and cling fast to the rail. Arthur, who was obviously badly hurt, lay where he had fallen, his eyes wild and his lips tightly closed with the effort not to cry out again.

I said, "We've got to get indoors".

Hunter said, "Are you all right, Arthur?"

Arthur said, "Imperative. Inside."

Before Hunter could untie the rope, the next wave took us. I held on to Arthur as tightly as I could, but even so he was cruelly buffeted, and by the time we had stumbled through the door with him, he was unconscious.

Inside the cabin, Gertrude, Sonya, Muriel, Tony and Mr. Banner had wrapped themselves round the legs of the table, which was screwed to the floor. Since Hunter's shutter things were not in position, all five of them had been soaked by the water which was slopping about inside. That there was comparatively so little of it was because those giant waves were too large to be bothered with the raft as an antagonist; it was no more to them than a speck on the water's surface.

I had time to carry Arthur to the bunk in the bedroom, and to throw myself across his body, gripping the sides of the bunk as tightly as I could with my arms and legs. The door to the bedroom had been latched back. Those to the galley and the bathroom were closed; behind the one could be heard the clash of saucepans, and I could guess that there would be broken glass behind the other. Most of the movable objects in the main cabin were books, and these damaged nothing but themselves as they were tossed about. Mr. Banner, struck on the ear by *Jamaica Inn,* went bravely on with his attempt to comfort and encourage the women under his charge. "Oh God," he said, "if it be indeed Thy design to punish us in this way for our misdeeds, be not too outrageous in Thy wrath. Spare, Oh Lord, the helpless. Bring succour to the distressed——" The plateglass port-hole in the wall beside me became momentarily part of the floor, and I could see the sea surging beneath the glass. Then we were in the calm again, and I shouted to Hunter to get the shutters up.

"You think we ought to?" he said.

"Arthur would wish it."

"Right ho," said Hunter. "Give us a hand, padre, will you?"

Mr. Banner unwound himself from the table leg. His face was grey-green from fear and nausea. Tony joined him. I told them to hurry while there was still time to move, and they stumbled over to the door. There the shutter was a kind of screen, which slid across and was secured by a bar. While Banner and Tony were dealing with the door, Hunter moved swiftly around the cabin, pulling down the shields of metal that reinforced the glass of the port-holes.

When they had finished, the cabin was in darkness, for Hunter had forgotten to turn on the light. The three men could not find their way back to the table. We heard them fall, and a bumping as they were thrown about. Then there was a cry from Gertrude.

After we were over the worst of it, I said, "Is everyone all right?"

"Hit my bloody head," said Hunter.

"Mr. Banner?" There was no reply. "*Banner!* Is he hurt? Can you find him in the dark?"

"Well, I don't think he's dead or anything, because he's just been sick," said Sonya. Banner groaned.

"Is he within reach?"

"Yes." I heard Sonya's voice, comforting in the temporary calm. "Here, hold on to me; you'll be all right. Goodness, don't *bother* about that."

"What have you done with my husband?" Muriel said.

There was no more calm after that for a long time. The giant waves were done, and what remained was simple tempest. The raft was battered and thrown from side to side while we lay in the darkness and wet of the cabin, listening to the waves and the wind. I lay closer to Arthur than a lover, keeping both him and myself on the bunk; my neck and arms and the backs of my knees ached with the tension. Ridiculously, I began to feel sea-sick, and so, I could hear, did the others; the cabin was filled with the stench, and became suffocatingly hot.

The suffocation and the stench. It was as if God had decided to take the intending suicide with his head in the gas-oven of a shabby basement flat, and give him a good shaking to bring him to his senses, but had neglected first to open the windows, so that Divine anger was only added to the physical discomforts a suicide has to bear already. In that close air, I seemed to see the whole raft caught up in God's hand to be rattled and shaken and tossed petulantly aside, falling again through the air, and turning over and over as it fell into a darkness that had no end. Down and down I fell through that darkness into sleep, knowing as I fell that it would be my last sleep, and sure enough, when I awoke we were at peace.

So I am dead, I thought. There was a sour taste in my mouth. My head ached, and my eyes were swollen; my body was stiff and sore. The cabin was hotter than ever. If this was Hell, it was only human discomfort aggravated a little. All things were the same, I noticed, save one— we were at peace. And when I groped for the shutter over the port-hole, and opened it, a shaft of sunlight illuminated the wall beyond.

7. *The Ark*

"Couldn't I have a drink of water?"

"I'm afraid not," Arthur said. "You are not allowed more than your ration."

"Ration?"

"We are becalmed, Mr. Clarke. The batteries are not charging, and will not until there is a wind again. I have instituted a strict rationing of all electrical power for the time being."

Inside the cabin pieces of cloth, moistened with sea water, had been draped over the port-holes for shade and coolness. Outside the sun shone steadily, and its rays were reflected upwards from the water, so that anyone on deck seemed to be caught in a cross-fire from the sun. All of us had burned and blistered except Hunter who was used to the sun and Arthur who, being already bruised a yellowish purple, could take no other colour.

On the second day of sunshine, I had come down with sunstroke, and now I lay on a bunk in the gloom of the cabin, drifting between sleep and waking, feverish, and with a steady pain at the back of my eyes, and Arthur visited me at regular intervals to take my temperature. "I don't know why you bother," I said. "You haven't any penicillin or anything. You can't bring it down."

"It does no harm to know," Arthur said, and he made a mark on the temperature chart he kept hidden from me in a folder.

"How is it going to end up, Arthur?"

"First the fever will go; in fact, I may as well tell you that it is already subsiding. Then you will be very weak for a little while, and——"

"I don't mean that. How are we going to end? All of us on board."

"Why, we shall survive, as I told you."

"I don't see how."

"That is because you have no vision." Arthur sat down on the side of the bunk. "Now that the rain has stopped, the waters will subside, and eventually we shall come to land. Then we must begin all over again."

"Without seed? Without livestock?"

"There is no alternative, Mr. Clarke. We must do what we can with what we have. I intend, when you have recovered, to call a meeting, and I shall put to them—I shall tell them— But let that keep; we must not anticipate. I shall survey our resources; I shall plan; everything will be arranged. Believe me, Mr. Clarke, I do not doubt that we shall survive. Taking the long view, there are no accidents in nature. Our survival so far has not been accidental; you cannot think that. Of course, we do not know how many other people may also have survived, where they may be, and what kind of people they may be. Such people may be our rivals. Survival in the natural order is often a matter of competition. Each group, each species, has certain advantages and opportunities. If we do not grasp our opportunities as they arise, we may not be judged fit to continue."

"Judged?"

"I use the word loosely, of course."

"I thought you never used words loosely."

"Sometimes. I have so many things to think of, so much to plan. My dear Mr. Clarke, you have no idea. It is not that I complain of strain; in work, man finds his justification. And if we are to begin Society all over again. . . ." He took off his spectacles, and I noticed that, now they were no longer shielded by the lenses, his eyes seemed a little out of focus. "What is man, Mr. Clarke?" he said. "Man is an animal with intelligence. That is his survival weapon. On the one hand, we must see that it is properly used as a weapon; that it is developed to the highest pitch of efficiency. And on the other, we must remember that it is only a weapon, if you understand me, and that it is to the welfare of man as an *animal* that our society must be devoted." He repeated the phrase slowly, "The welfare of man as an animal."

"I've never thought of you as an animal, Arthur."

He ran his tongue over his lips. "There you make your mistake," he said. "Because a man fits himself to lead. . . . But that, you see, is precisely—I do not often share my thoughts, Mr. Clarke; it is not a characteristic of leadership. But I have been thinking a great deal. Imagination, you see, is the enemy. There is no place for that. We shall not be concerned, therefore, with gods or devils; there is no place for the supernatural."

"But you've always encouraged Banner to say Grace."

"Many arrangements that govern our existence on this raft must be jettisoned once we are ashore. An element of formality at this time gives shape to lives that are in danger of being made shapeless by *ennui*. But once we have landed, there will be plenty to do; everyone will see that, you may be sure. We shall have no time for dreams. An animal does not allow itself to dream, for if it does, it dies."

My head ached. "Look," I said. "What's the point of living without imagination? Or without God or whatever? You've got to have a point. Look at all those tribes in the South Seas that just died out. Look at all the people who commit suicide. It isn't keeping alive that makes one want to live; it's the trimmings that go with it."

"I shall not allow anyone to die out," Arthur said. "I shall not allow it. You talk of suicides. A suicide is a neurotic by definition, and neuroses of any sort spring from the imagination, Mr. Clarke. It is the fifth column. We must stamp it out. Don't you see, it is all part of the test. Imagination, you may say, exists within us like a cancer. When we have destroyed it, we shall have proved ourselves worthy of survival."

"Test . . . prove . . . worthy," I said. "You make the whole thing sound like an entrance examination."

"If it will encourage you, Mr. Clarke, let me tell you that I have never failed an examination in my life." He smiled, put on his spectacles, and patted the sheet paternally. "We must talk again," he said. "Intelligent discussion is a great stimulus to me. But perhaps you should rest now. I have already excited you too much." And he rose briskly from the bunk, and left the room, taking the temperature chart with him.

After he had gone, I lay in the gloom of the darkened cabin, and my head ached. All this talk about survival, when there was so much against us. I thought about the batteries, no longer charging. What should we do when we could no longer distil drinking water? And food? How long could we exist on Glub and fish? Even if we were to come to land, what then? We had no seed! No livestock! Even the International Unitarian Breakfast Food Company did not suggest that Glub was self-propagating. And tools? Would Intelligence conjure a plough for us out of the mud of some eventual island? Clothes? We were wearing trunks and bikinis improvised from Hunter's spare shirts, and when they wore out, I supposed we should go naked like animals, like Arthur's intelligent animals, whom he would lead, naked and without possessions, into the Promised Land.

All right; so all right, I thought. We're going to survive the voyage, and we're going to reach land, and there'll be enough to eat, and we'll settle down together to make a fresh start for the human race. And what kind of job shall we make of it? What shall we teach our children?— what do we know between the eight of us?—what of medicine, chemistry, engineering? Who are we to make a fresh start, I thought. Even if Arthur were preposterously right, and Nature had selected us, what a poor selection the silly lady had made! In this sort of picking a new team, the convention was to begin with the scientists, just as the first of the books one took to a desert island in the newspaper competitions was always the Bible, because it was holy and because it was long. Once upon a time, I thought, there were a doctor, a chemist, a farmer and an electrical engineer, and they took four healthy girls with degrees from the University of London, and settled down together on a desert island, where they were very happy and founded the New Jerusalem. But not us. Not Arthur Renshaw, Sonya Banks, Gertrude Harrison, Muriel Otterdale, Geoffrey Hunter, Harold Banner, Tony Ryle and John Clarke. Why, even the balance of the sexes was uneven, unless Arthur intended to reintroduce a celibate priesthood among his rational animals.

And yet we could not live except by the belief that in some way we should survive; otherwise we might as well start now to decide upon the least unpleasant way of dying. If Arthur's dottiness about our being intelligent animals would keep us going, I had better encourage it. Arthur was a good sort of man, and an excellent nurse, in spite of his formality and fussiness. His insistence on "Visiting Hours" had led to my practical isolation for most of the time. Even Sonya's visits had been restricted. I found myself obsessively concerned to know how she was passing the time. How long ago was it since she had come to see me? When would she come again? What did they do out there all day long, those intelligent animals under Arthur's command?

Faintly from outside the port I could hear their voices. Gertrude's laugh. Sonya: "Tony's got a fabulous tan when you consider he was all pink and peeling two days ago." Banner: a phrase in which I caught the words, "the sons of Ham". Then Sonya again: "Well, you're not to send him out into the wilderness just because he's darker than the rest of us. I won't have it." And nearer at hand (they must have been passing just underneath the port as they strolled on deck together), Muriel's voice: "Of course we'd always do anything you told us to, Arthur. You know that."

I closed my eyes again, and turned to face the wall of

the cabin. Encourage Arthur, I thought; Arthur did not
need encouragement from me or from any of us. Like
Muriel, I would do what Arthur commanded, because of
us all only Arthur knew where he was going. And for all
my civilized reservations, I had neither the will to oppose
him, nor the vision to lead in his place.

I recovered, and lay on the deck in the sun with the
others. The sun shone, and the air was still. Arthur called
a meeting, and we elected him President of the New Society, nemine contra dicente. He told us we should each
have a part to play, and that in the meantime he would
continue to make rules that should govern our conduct
on board. I asked whether there was any provision for a
Deputy in case anything should happen to him; Arthur
replied that nothing was likely to happen to him. There
being no further business, the meeting ended.

We lay becalmed, and the sun shone steadily down. We
had hoisted sail, but there was no wind to fill it; a lug
sail, it hung from the mast like old washing. We had no
idea how far the storm had carried us, knew that we were
in the northern hemisphere, but could not tell if we were
over Switzerland or the Atlantic Ocean, for none of us
had skill with the stars. From the length of the nights, we
could judge that we had not reached either the tropics or
the Arctic Circle.

The heat made us languorous, and Arthur's conserving
the batteries was an inconvenience. We washed and
shaved in cold salt water, which left us sticky; Banner and
I in particular were corrugated with cuts. We ate once a
day only, a mess of stewed fish and Glub. Fish, indeed,
were abundant, and many were of kinds we could not
recognize; once we caught a strange creature, half-eel, half-
dragon, which, skinned and then broiled on the electric
plate of the stove, proved to have flesh as succulent as
veal. During the nights the water shone with phosphorescence, and the fish would come up to sport on the surface. Silver-green and silver-blue, they would leap in the
air or chase each other the length of the raft; sometimes

the same fish might seem to be swimming ceaselessly round and round us as if curious to examine so unfishy a fellow-traveller.

One morning when Gertrude and I were first out of the cabin, we found a seal lying on deck, basking belly upwards in the sun. Gertrude gripped my arm. "Don't tell Arthur," she said. "He will want to kill it for food." Slowly, but with a beautiful sureness in her gait, she approached the seal, and laid her hand on its head. The seal's whiskers twitched under the shadow of her arm, and I believed it purred. It lay there quite still, allowing her to stroke it while I stood apart, until the cabin door opened and we were joined by Banner. Instantly the seal dived overboard, and, as I glanced at Gertrude, I saw that there were tears in her eyes.

Arthur, when Banner told him of the seal's visit, was pleased with Gertrude. "It is clear that you have a way with animals, my dear," he said. "I am sure we shall be able to make use of it." I had never heard him call any of us but by our given names, and Gertrude was almost as pleased by the "my dear", I think, as by his praise.

That was the happiest time of the voyage. In the bright sunlight, it was almost as if we were on an extended houseboat holiday, with Arthur as scoutmaster-in-charge. The diet was meagre, the living conditions spartan, but that was to be expected. It was so pleasant to be warm again, and dry, and, now that the blistering and the sunstroke were over, to lie like lizards soaking up the sunlight, and in the evenings to watch the great set-pieces of green, and orange and violet that were our sunsets. Arthur kept telling us that we must fit ourselves to become citizens of the New Society, but this seemed to mean no more than that we must perform the tasks he set us. We ourselves never thought about the New Society, and our talk was of the world as we had known it far more than of the future. We lived from day to day, and were contented. We had resigned our wills to Arthur, and were no more than engines, not yet harnessed, lying in readiness for the time when their creator would put them to use.

And we were healthy enough at that time, in a low-keyed way; we had not yet begun to suffer from short commons and too little water. We were healthy, with one exception. Muriel had gone broody since her husband's death. Where the rest of us were obedient, she was servile. There was something suspect and fawning about her manner to Arthur, something possessive as if they shared some shameful secret from which the rest of us were excluded.

"No," Banner said, "It is true I had no vocation, but I thought I might be able to do some good in the world."

We were lying on deck, Gertrude and Banner stretched out in the sunshine, myself in the scanty shade the sail afforded. Somewhere below us in the hold, Sonya was doing her *barre* and Tony lifting his weights or bending himself backwards over a piece of board. Arthur was writing up the log in the cabin, while Muriel watched him. Hunter was fishing.

Banner said, "Like Captain Hunter, I was never cut out for an office job."

Gertrude propped herself on her elbows, and said seriously, "A free soul needs expression, Harold. How well I know that."

"Yes, I suppose so," Banner said. "I wanted to do something."

"Ah, the Life Lie," I said.

"Life Lie?"

"Ibsen," Gertrude said. "*The Wild Duck*. A hopeless, hopeless message," and she sighed.

Banner said, "I don't understand."

I said, "Well, Ibsen's thesis in *The Wild Duck* is that everyone needs a lie to live by. Whatever Arthur may say, most human beings are not absolute fools. They know that human life is a pretty pointless business. They are born, and grow old, and die. They eat and drink, and go to work

every day, and take one, two or three weeks' holiday every
year. They raise children, and the children grow up and
leave home, and the parents are left alone. Much of their
life is spent in pain, and more in boredom, and most in
indifference. All they have to expect is monotony and
struggle for most of their working lives, and loneliness and
fear in their old age. And what's it all for? They don't
really believe that making things, and packing them in
cans or boxes, and loading them in cars and ships and
planes, and transporting them, and writing advertising
copy about them, and selling them, and buying them, and
using them, and disposing of what is left, and making new
things to replace them are ends in themselves. Yet if life
is to be tolerable, they must believe in some sort of purpose to it, and that's where the Life Lie comes in. A religious vocation, dedicating oneself to the good of society,
adding to the store of human knowledge, painting a picture or writing a book, winning battles or finding a cure
for cancer—it doesn't matter what it is as long as you
believe it, Ibsen would say. But of course once you recognize your need for a Life Lie, once you write about it or
talk about it or bring it out into the front of your mind,
then it becomes more difficult to find a Life Lie that will
work for you, because it is only a lie after all, and once
you know that, it has no power any more, and all is emp-
tiness again."

"I don't follow you," Banner said.

Gertrude said, "I do. Sometimes when I was feeling
lonely, I would lie awake in Earl's Court, you know, and
wonder whether it was all worth while. But I had to
decide that it was, or I could never have carried on. It
is a wicked play in that way, *The Wild Duck*."

"But it didn't arise," said Banner. "Of course it seemed
worth while. I wanted to help people."

"Why didn't you become a social worker?" I said.

"The qualifications."

Gertrude said, "What qualifications? A free heart, an
open hand—surely that is all you need?"

"Some sort of degree in Social Science, I believe," Banner said. "I had thought I would like to be a probation officer, but when I made inquiries, they would not take me. I was too young at that time, and lacked the proper academic background—I got a fourth, you know. It was not good enough to qualify me as a probation officer, but the Church of England was not so particular. Although of course I had to undergo further training in a seminary at St. Andrews."

"But how did you——?"

"Begin? I suppose you might say I drifted into it— an apt enough method for a rowing man. I was given my Blue, you see, in my second year. Nobody had taken very much notice of me up to that time, but the Moral Rearmament people were keen to recruit athletic personalities; they believed that where we showed the way, the good college men would follow. They sent a chap round to see me, and he asked me to tea. There was a Rugger Blue and a Cricket Blue and a Boxing Blue and two peers and a don from St. Peter's Hall. We had strawberries and cream, and confessed our sins. I had never gone in for that kind of thing before, and it did seem interesting."

"You didn't stay with that lot surely."

"No. I was too bashful. I found the greatest difficulty in confessing even to very tiny faults. After all, if the faults were small, it seemed presumptuous to expect people to be interested, and if they were large I would rather keep them to myself. And you know, I didn't greatly care for the people. So I dropped away after a bit, (though I'm bound to say they kept sending me very friendly letters) and confined myself to the University Christian Union; even that I began to find a bit evangelical, but I felt it better to keep in touch. And then when I began to consider ordination seriously, they were a great help."

"How did you manage to swallow it all?" I said.

"Swallow what?"

"If you didn't have a vocation, how did you manage to swallow all the dogma?"

"It didn't seem important somehow," Banner said. "There is a far wider latitude of belief in the Church of England than most people think. I had no more objection to conducting a service than I had to attending one; there was just rather more to say. After all, although my views have grown broader than they were, I'm not a heathen, you know."

"No, of course not."

"I simply wanted to do some good. And as a clergyman, I found that people came to me for advice, and then there were the Youth Clubs, and I was able to help in resettling some of my parishioners who'd had the misfortune to spend time in prison, and the days went by very swiftly. I was so busy that I had little time to think about religious questions, and when I did, you know, I discovered that most things were explicable in simple terms. All those doubts people used to have! There was never any need for them, since the Sunday papers have proved that virgin birth is perfectly possible, and most of the miracles have been duplicated by scientists. In any case, I wasn't required to be a fundamentalist. Nobody wanted me to believe in God as a person, or in Christ as anything else. Nowadays, you know, Heaven is not a place, but a oneness with God; the individual soul dissolves into the God-soul, as it were—not very easy to communicate to one's parishioners, but then one's contact with them is not in church; one never sees them in church, and all the good work is done in the Clubs and on the playing fields."

"But the beauty of it. The stillness. The communion," Gertrude said. "One has to believe in that."

Banner said, "Oh, I don't know. It's not a thing I ever experienced, you see, except in other people's churches sometimes, older than mine, and more—more foreign like Notre Dame or St. Peter's. My church was a nineteenth-century construction in an industrial parish, and the choir

—I don't think I ever had more than six in the choir or sixty in the congregation."

At the edge of the raft, Hunter suddenly stood up, jerked his fishing line out of the water, and shouted, "Land ho!"

It was not land. It was an ark.

We could not know this. We could see no more than its indistinct outline against the horizon. Long before Hunter sighted it, the ark must have been lying as we were, becalmed in the smooth sea, for it did not come any closer to us, nor could we approach it. Both ark and raft remained where they were, and the whole party of us, gathered on deck in response to Hunter's call, strained our eyes to stare at it, still thinking it to be land.

"It might be a mirage," I said.

"And it might not."

"Hadn't you better send out a dove?" I said.

Muriel said, "You've no reason to mock," and Arthur took off his glasses, and wiped them on the side of his trunks. "Are there any binoculars on board, Captain Hunter?" he said.

"Oh Lord," said Hunter, "I can't remember where I left them."

"Try," Arthur said, "And while you are trying, the rest of us will return to whatever we were doing. Mr. Ryle, if you have finished your exercises, perhaps you will take a turn at fishing." He went back to the cabin, and Muriel followed him. The rest of us, once the door was safely closed, continued to stare out to sea.

When the binoculars had been found, Arthur stood for some time, gazing through them at the distant shape. "It is a vessel," he said.

"Any sign of life?"

"None. But at this distance one can distinguish very little." Arthur lowered the binoculars, and put them away in their case. Nobody else asked to use them; they had already become a badge of leadership like an officer's sword. "We shall have to go and see," he said.

"How?"

"The dinghy."

The dinghy and paddles were still in the hold. "I'll go," Hunter said.

"Wait," Arthur said. "It is too far to paddle this afternoon; we should not be able to return in daylight. Captain Hunter, are you sure there are no other weapons on board beside your fishing spear?"

"Sorry, Arthur."

Gertrude said, "Weapons?"

"Miss Harrison, you must not assume that everyone has the same gentleness of spirit as yourself. If that should be a vessel as I think it, and if there should be a crew aboard, we may be attacked. We have food, which they may covet. We have seen them; perhaps they have also seen us. We must not rule out the possibility of piracy."

"But Arthur," Banner said, "surely at a time like this we're all in the same boat?"

"Manifestly not, Mr. Banner. We are in our boat, they in theirs. If ours is the more seaworthy, they may wish to make an exchange. We shall mount a guard tonight."

That night Banner, Hunter, Tony and I stood watches. I do not know whether the others felt as foolish as I did as I paced around the deck, staring over the moonlit water. Together the moon and the phosphorescence made a silver world, so that it was easy to believe in the mermaids and sea-sirens who would coax a man down the silver walk to the ocean's depths. And then? I stopped, my eyes turned inward, as I tried to decide which was more likely, the bleached bones on the siren's rocks or the friendly underwater world of an E. Nesbit story in the *Strand* magazine.

"Have you had quiet guard?" Banner asked, coming to relieve me.

"Not a shrimp stirring." Nevertheless I dreamed of wet mermen that night, their heads covered with spotted

scarves, cutlasses between their teeth, their eyes red and
bloody, water dripping from their scales and their wild
hair as they pulled themselves onto the raft from the
shining sea.

Next morning we were ready to make up a boarding
party, but Arthur had changed his mind. He did not wish,
he said, to split our forces if there were any danger of
having to fight. Instead he spent the day watching the
other vessel through the binoculars, and by the evening
he had decided it was deserted.

We stood guard that night also just the same, and in
the morning we made ready for the expedition. Arthur
himself would go with us; Hunter and I would paddle.
"Darling," Sonya said to me while she and I inflated
the dinghy. "Could there really be anyone there?"

"Arthur doesn't think so."

"But there might be?"

"I suppose."

She twitched her nose in thought. "Here, wait a sec,"
she said, and went inside the cabin. When she returned,
she had brought her little silver Christopher. She gave it to
me. "I don't believe in taking chances," she said.

I said, "Oh, darling!" and Sonya said, "Well . . ." and
Arthur came out of the cabin and told us to hurry.

We set off. Arthur sat in the dinghy, and Hunter and
I took up the paddles. We began to move away, watched
by the others who had gathered on deck to see us go.
The women put up their hands to wave. "Good luck,
good luck!" Banner cried.

As the distance widened between us, for the first time
I saw the raft in the context of the water that surrounded
it, and realized how small it was, our floating home, which
had seemed roomy and secure enough when we were on
board. Now, on all that waste of water, there were only
the raft and this other vessel on the horizon and the tiny
rubber dinghy crossing from one to the other. It was going
to be painful crossing for me, I realized. Already the
muscles of my arms and shoulders were aching, and as

the sweat dripped into my eyes from my forehead, I began to feel dizzy. "Take ten," Arthur said suddenly, and we rested.

We toiled on under the hot sun towards the vessel, and as we drew nearer we could see its outlines more clearly. It really did look as if it had been built from a model in a child's picture book of Noah. There were open pieces of deck at the prow and stern, but the rest was covered with a peaked roof, partly torn away by the gale, and the ark rode high in the water, and lopsidedly as if the cargo were badly stowed. Nothing moved on board. Arthur shouted, "Ahoy! Ahoy there!" and the sound died on the open water without reply. He shouted again. The rubber dinghy bumped against the side of the ark. "Christ!" Hunter said, "what a pong!"

It was true; the stench was horrible. "Something has died," Arthur said. "Will you see if you can find a place to tie up, Mr. Clarke?" We paddled all round the ark, and found nothing, nor was there any sign of occupation other than the stench. "Perhaps if Captain Hunter were to hoist you on his shoulders, Mr. Clarke, you would be able to climb on board," Arthur said. I climbed up, and pulled Arthur after me. We stood uncertainly on the empty deck at the prow, and Arthur shouted again, "Is anyone here?" This time we thought we heard a faint reply from the interior. There was a door in front of us, and I opened it.

Through the open door, the stench came out to overwhelm us. It was like something living, like warm flesh suddenly released from the constriction of a corset. I gave way before it, and rushing to the side, was immediately sick; Arthur stayed where he was. Nothing else could be alive inside, I thought; there would not be room. But there was something. It appeared in the doorway, blinking against the light, its mouth and eyes opening contrapuntally. But no sound came from the mouth, and the eyes were red in a face encrusted with filth, and set in a frame of matted hair. Arthur said, "Get the water bottle," and when I had hoisted it from the dinghy, and we had laid the scarecrow man down in the shade, and fed him gently with water, he spoke to us, and said, "They all died; they all died."

"Your livestock?"

"Yes. There was no water. And they had fouled their quarters. I saved . . . saved grain," he said. "I saved it for food and seed. Some of it was spoiled by the storm, and afterwards there was no water. There had been so much before. I could not think of everything."

"You had better take a look round, Mr. Clarke," Arthur said.

"I have drunk blood," said the man. "Ham, Shem—both dead. My wife left me, you know, before the Word was fulfilled; she took Japhet, and went to her married sister in Ruislip. When we were very thirsty, we drank the blood of our Shetland pony, but the two boys died. More has occurred than was foretold."

"Where is the grain?" Arthur said.

"Inside. And the seeds in tins. Flowers too. Beauty should not vanish from the earth. I bought nasturtiums since they were cheap, and marigolds, and London Pride. No gardens without flowers."

"Let me know what you find, Mr. Clarke," Arthur said.

Getting through that door was like walking into a grave. Each forward step I took built up the force within me that wanted to turn and run out again. I tried to cover my nose and mouth against the stench, breathing through the chinks between my fingers, but it did little good.

All the interior of the ark was one large room. The animals lay there, dead in their stalls, their bodies already bloated with decay and filthy with ordure. To one end were piled sacks of grain and roots; the rain had rotted them, but I could see a number of bins that must contain seed, and the contents of these would be in good condition. I made a move to open them, but before I could reach the bins I felt my dizziness begin again, and knew that I should faint if I did not return to the deck outside.

I made my report to Arthur. "Can we carry the bins away with us?" he asked.

"Not really. They'd sink the dinghy."

"Very well. We must devise something else."

"What about the man?"

"He is in no state to be moved," Arthur said. "You can see that for yourself. Let us make him comfortable where he is."

"And come back for him?"

"Unless you would care to stay."

"I don't think I could," I said. "The stench . . . I suppose he's grown used to it."

"Yes."

I bent over the man. "Look," I said. "We're going away now, but we'll come back tomorrow. We're going to leave the water bottle with you. We'll bring food when we come." The man did not reply; he had talked himself out, it seemed. But he stared up at me, and his eyes blinked, and I think he would have nodded his head if he could.

We returned to the raft more quickly than we had come. Except when he gave the order to rest, Arthur was silent, his lips tightly pressed together in thought. When the journey was almost over, he said, "I have decided. We cannot bring the grain to the raft as easily as we can tow the raft to the grain. We shall do it tomorrow."

In fact, it was not a task that could be finished in one day; my promise to the scarecrow man was broken. First there was the straining and sweating at the paddles of the dinghy to get the raft to move at all; then, even after our effort had become effective, it could not be diminished, for the raft never gathered enough speed through the water to allow us to rest for a while as it coasted. We all took turns, even Arthur himself, in shifts of four while a leader chanted the time of the strokes. We rested only at night and during the fiercest heat of the day.

I did not expect the man still to be alive when, on the third day, we reached the ark, but he was. He lay where we had left him, and when he saw me he only said, "You were here before." The water bottle was empty, and we gave him more, and the women brought sacking to make him more comfortable, and fed him with the fish stew that was our usual diet. The men, under Arthur's direction, transhipped what of the ark's cargo could be useful to us. When we had finished, the light was almost gone. "We must pull away a little for the night," Arthur said. "This is not a healthy atmosphere to sleep in."

Again in the dusk we strained to set the raft in motion, and took up our station about thirty yards away. "That should be enough," Arthur said. That night, as on the two nights before it, we went to bed as soon as we had eaten, falling asleep almost on the instant.

At perhaps two o'clock in the morning, I awoke from a dream of flames as Arthur stepped on my foot. He made his way to his own place, and lay down; I could see him clearly in the flickering orange light that filled the cabin, as I could see the sleeping faces of Banner, Hunter and Tony Ryle. I rose and went to the cabin door; Arthur half turned on his pallet, and I knew he was watching me. I went out on deck. The sky was bright with orange and yellow light from the burning ark. The fire had taken hold of the great central storehouse that we had rifled so short a while before, and the flames jumped high in the air from the hole in the roof, lighting up the whole of the forward deck where, it seemed to me, I could see the scarecrow man, his arms spread wide, his head flung back. He stood there for a moment like the figurehead of a doomed vessel. Then a dragon's tongue of flame came from the open door behind him, licked him once, and he was gone.

Muriel stood beside me on the deck. My face was

scorched, my throat dry. "He murdered him," I said. "Arthur murdered him."

"Oh yes," Muriel said. "My husband too. Arthur takes what he wants. After all, he has to, hasn't he, if we're all to respect him?"

She turned, and walked inside the cabin. The sky grew brighter as the flames spread over the whole of the ark. Somewhere in the heart of the fire there was an explosion. A baulk of wood, flung high into the air, came flaming towards us like a shooting-star, fell just short of the side of the raft, and disappeared. Then, with a long hiss as the burning wood touched the face of the water, the ark sank.

8. Becalmed

One of the beliefs that we used to hold in the Army was that the Authorities put saltpetre in the N.A.A.F.I. tea, and by that means prevented the more lustful among us from running wild; a counter view was that the hard work and exercise to which we were not accustomed had the same effect. Meanwhile near any Army Camp the bushes bloomed with limp rubber sheaths, and the bellies of a few unlucky local girls began to swell; neither saltpetre nor exercise, it seemed, were enough in themselves to destroy desire.

Arthur had no saltpetre with which to dose us, and the work was light as we lay becalmed, but of course we were not very well nourished; at any rate he had no trouble with us in that way. One falls so quickly into a habit of living. It was not making love to Sonya that I missed, but something much more important to me, that feeling of being together which we had shared in the dinghy, but which now seemed to have been lost. We were no longer a pair, it seemed to me, but part of a group of eight; I felt that I had no more part in Sonya than the others had. "We're never alone together nowadays," I said, as we cleaned fish in the galley for the evening meal.

"We're alone now."

"Not really. Someone might come in."

"Do you want us to be alone?"

"Of course I do."

"What do you want to talk about?"

"I don't want to talk about anything. I just want to be with you."

"You're with me all the time."

"Oh, never mind."

"Well," Sonya said, "if you're going to go off at me about it. . . ." She put down her knife, and wiped her fishy hands on her bikini. Then she led me out on deck, and down the ladder into the hold. At the bottom of the ladder she turned and faced me. "We're alone now," she said. "You needn't worry about being overheard, if you don't shout."

"But we're not. . . ."

"What?"

"You can't just be alone," I said. "You have to be in the mood. It's a state of mind."

"All right," she said. "Let's go back. When you're in the mood for being alone, we can come down here again."

I said, "You don't understand."

"Yes I do," Sonya said, "you are a fool. Do I have to ask you to kiss me, or what?" I took her face between my hands, and kissed her. Her body pressed against mine, and my arms slid down her back. I swayed, and very nearly fell over. "I think we'd better sit down," I said.

As we lay on the floor together, Sonya snuggled into me, shivering a little under my exploring hands. For some time we lay there, silent. Then she said, "Do you think I don't miss you?"

I kissed her again passionately, and she placed my hand back on her shoulders. "Not now," she said, "it's not important."

"But——"

"After all, it's only sex," she said. "We can have that at any time. Let's just be together now."

"But a moment ago——"

"You were being stupid about it, and I got angry," she said. "Do you think I haven't been feeling the same way? I never have any part of you; you're always with the others, and you all talk and talk, and I get bored. But I couldn't tell you I wanted to get away from them; you had to ask me, and you never did. I used to come down here every day to practise with Tony, and I kept wondering when you'd see——"

"With Tony?"

"Well, of course. We only use it for practising, and the rest of the time it's empty. Nobody ever comes here."

My hand, which had been stroking her shoulder, stopped, and lay still. "I think we ought to be getting back on deck," I said, "they'll miss us."

"Who cares if they do?"

"Arthur wouldn't like it." I kissed her again gently. "Come on, darling," I said. "He'll only make a rule about it if he finds out. We can come again."

Sonya said, "All right," and I helped her to get to her feet. We held hands as we walked across to the foot of the ladder. I had to walk a little wide to avoid Tony's improvised weights. *After all it's only sex*, I thought, and then, *I come down here with Tony every day.*

At the top of the ladder, just before we were visible from the deck, Sonya bent down and kissed me on the mouth. "You are strange, you know," she said, and we walked back to the galley in silence.

Soon we began to be on what Arthur called "strict water discipline"; he seemed to enjoy the phrase, which was a hang-over from his days with the Rajputana Rifles during the war. As well as cutting down on water, he took all the bulbs out of the light sockets, and locked them away in a drawer; there were to be no more readings and discussions in the cabin after supper. Everything moved so slowly in those days: the needle in Muriel's hand describing a slow arc from one stitch to the next, the lazy progress of a broom across the galley floor, the barb of a fish-hook sinking like a wire through ice into the belly of the small fish Hunter would be using for bait. We moved through time as if it were treacle, and lay for most of the day on deck under the improvised awning of a sail, waiting in the heat for a breeze.

Once upon a time, when I had said, "I'm hungry," it

had not meant that I was in pain. I had thought that "the pangs of hunger" meant no more than "the pangs of love"; a stale metaphor for need. But now I discovered that hunger was a physical sensation, an intermittent gnawing pain in the upper belly. We could rely on its visits; like a faithful creditor it came always at the same time in the afternoon. Hunger was a beast, to be mollified. We could not give it food, but we tried to stroke it into harmlessness. Round and round over the skin of our bellies our hands would pass to soothe and smooth away the pangs.

Since we ate a stew of fish and Glub in the evenings, our hunger was not constant, but thirst was always with us as a stickiness in the mouth and throat. We drank twice a day, never more than a couple of mouthfuls, and there was liquid in our evening stew, but however much they may have nourished our bodies, these rationed mouthfuls did nothing to make us feel less thirsty, and as inactivity and the heat sucked talk out of us during those days on deck, our tongues seemed to increase in size until they filled our mouths like blotting paper.

When I remember this time, it seems that Arthur always sat apart in the cabin, writing and writing in the blank volumes of the log; perhaps he liked to be near the water jar. Hunter took over the fishing completely. He would sit all day on the edge of the raft, his limbs slack, his head lolling a little. The sun did not affect Hunter, except as a drug; his reactions had slowed and his initiative almost disappeared, so that once when he left his post to visit the privy, we found him still there some two hours later, sitting with the vacant expression he always wore and that only a pull on the float could disturb.

Tony and Sonya still went every day into the hold to practise. I did not know what they did there. At about the same time every afternoon, Tony would say, "Coming, Sonn?" and they would climb down the ladder, and I would watch them go, and remember my own last visit to the hold with Sonya, and try to push away the doubts and questions that came into my mind.

We were hungry and thirsty, and still the sun shone, and the air was still. Our batteries gave power but did not get it as we lay idle in the water. Hunter said that he had never known them to give out, but he admitted that he had not been becalmed so long before. The arrow on the dial of the ammeter crept slowly backwards, and the days went by.

"It is no good," Arthur said. "We are still using too much power. We must cut down."

"Cut down," Muriel said. Much of Muriel's conversation now was to repeat what had just been spoken.

"We waste power in the cooking."

"I'm sorry, Arthur," I said, "I don't use more than I can help."

"I am sure you do not, Mr. Clarke. But you misunderstand me. With the situation as it is, it would be better not to use any power at all in cooking."

"Just eat Glub?"

"That would not be practical without moisture of some sort. I suppose, Captain Hunter, that there is no supply of *liquid* Glub that we have overlooked?"

"There's Glub in a Matchbox."

I said, "It has to be chewed slowly to set the rich nourishing juices circulating through the system. We can't just swallow it."

"Has to be chewed," Muriel said.

"I see. Well perhaps we might try Glub in a Matchbox two nights a week, increasing the water ration a little so as to allow us to chew. For the other evenings we must make shift with our fish *au bleu*."

"Blue?"

"Raw."

"Eat raw fish?"

"Others have done so. It should be cut up to release the moisture, and the scales removed. Very much, in fact, as you usually prepare it, but uncooked."

We began on our new diet next evening. Banner asked a blessing, and we dipped our spoons into the mess. There they remained for a while, and each looked at the others to see who would be the first to taste it. Arthur lifted his spoon to his mouth, and swallowed a spoonful of fish. "It is unpleasant on the whole," he said.

Banner said, "The Japanese consider it a delicacy." His face twitched with disgust as he tasted the fish, but he swallowed it, and one by one we followed his example.

Only Sonya did not. She lowered her spoon, and sat with her head hanging, staring at her plate. "I can't eat it," she said, "I'll be sick."

"Come now, Miss Banks," Arthur said, "it will do you good."

"It won't do me any good if I bring it all up again."

"You must keep it down."

"I can't. I don't want any. Anybody can have my share."

Arthur tapped his spoon upon his plate, and gazed round the table. "There is no need for us all to stop eating just because Miss Banks is having a little difficulty with her fish," he said. With his prim mouth and glittering spectacles, he looked like a nanny presiding at nursery tea. "Come now, Miss Banks," he said. "You must eat your fish. Let us try again."

"Must eat our nice fish," said Muriel.

"I can't," Sonya said. I could hear tears in her voice.

I said, "If she doesn't want it, I don't see why anyone should force her to eat it. After all, it's her own funeral."

"Exactly, Mr. Clarke. If Miss Banks does not eat, that will be her own funeral. And while she is under my charge, I do not intend that her funeral shall take place."

"Can't she have Glub and water instead?"

"There will be no exceptions."

"Darling," I said, "try to eat some. It's easier once you get started."

Sonya lifted her head, and stared at me. I could see that her eyes were angry behind the tears. "I don't see why you've got to interfere," she said.

"Quite right. There is no reason at all for Mr. Clarke to interfere."

"I'm sorry, Arthur."

"Sorrow by itself means nothing unless it is accompanied by the intention of amendment. Do not interfere again."

"No. I won't."

"Then we shall continue with our meal. Miss Banks, I appreciate how you feel. The fish is indeed nauseous at first taste, and no good would be done at all if, after swallowing, you were to vomit it up again. If you wish, I shall ask Mrs. Otterdale to hold your nose while you eat."

We were all quite silent now. Muriel began to rise from her place, but Arthur waved her back. "We shall avoid it if we can," he said. Sonya took her first mouthful of raw fish, and followed it very quickly with a second. Arthur took a mouthful. We copied him obediently. Soon we were eating in unison, our spoons rising and falling a little after Arthur's, and when it came to the end, our plates were cleared together.

Now the tigers of jealousy began to invade my mind, and I was too weak to keep them out.

Company would have helped to keep the tigers away, but I shunned company, lying for long hours on the deck feigning sleep, turning my face away from the others and hugging my arms close to my chest as if I loved the tigers and wanted to keep them with me always. And the tigers would walk through my mind endlessly, delicately, waving their tails and conjuring up pictures for me. The tigers themselves did not rend me, but the pictures they made were hurtful.

Jealousy needs no nourishment from outside. The memory of a long-past indiscretion, a misheard sentence—the tigers need only a single puff of air to give them life, and after that they make their own. For almost as long as I had lived, these tigers had lurked below the surface of

my mind, awaiting only the excuse for life, and now they
had it. They were my tigers. They were part of me. Bone,
flesh and pelt were made out of my own insecurities, my
own deep knowledge that I was not a person to be loved
easily, or sincerely, or for long. *Haply that I am black*—
disaster would have come in some way to Othello, even
if Iago had never existed. Iago was no more than a trigger.
He was a conceited man, as well as wicked, to imagine
otherwise.

I lay on the deck in the sun apart from the others, and
the pictures made by the tigers followed one another
through my mind. Sometimes I would accuse Sonya; I
would come right out and accuse her, and she would
laugh at me cruelly, saying, "Well, really I don't see why
you should think you're the only one," and again, "It's
just sex after all." Sometimes I would tackle the two of
them together, and what a scene would follow! Anger!
recrimination! remorse! regret! each of the tigers' pictures
came complete with dialogue, superbly theatrical, superbly
final. I walked out on Sonya and the curtain fell forty
times a day, always to rise again on the next picture, and
the next, and the next, while the playful tigers purred
and paraded interminably in my mind.

I wanted so much to turn my suspicions into knowledge. I wanted so much to go down and surprise them
in the hold, but I was frightened. What if they were
indeed—what if they were? Whatever unrelenting dialogue
the tigers might give me to speak, I loved Sonya, and
that could not be changed. I could not leave her confined
as we were, it was in any case impossible to do so except
by death. If I were to find out for certain, I should become
the complaisant cuckold of the French stories, despicable
in all men's eyes, and in my own (the tigers gave me that
picture also). And suppose I were to find nothing? It
would shame me to be spying on them, and would not
quiet the tigers.

My behaviour changed. I found myself alternating
between moods of sullenness and moods when I would

be impossibly placatory with Sonya, for I could no longer take our day-to-day life together for granted. Even Arthur noticed how strangely I was behaving. I think he believed that I might be "cracking up", because he kept finding extra tasks for me, so that my mind might be occupied.

Coming one afternoon from polishing the galley stove for the third time in four days, I found that Muriel was watching me. She sat on deck in my usual place near Gertrude and Banner, and, when she saw that I had noticed her, she smiled a thin smile and glanced in the direction of the ladder which led down into the hold. Sonya and Tony would be practising, doing their exercises, doing—what might they be doing together in the hold? I paused by the top of the ladder, listened, and could hear no sound of voices. Why were they so silent? But it was bettter, I thought, it was better for them to be silent. Let Tony be in my place, let him do—and let her. . . . Let them both do the action, but let me keep the words. Let Sonya not say to anyone else the special loving words we used with each other, let her not cry out, let her not. . . . But perhaps these words were as automatic a part of the act as orgasm itself. Like chocolate from a slot machine, out they came when you pressed the right handle.

Muriel was still watching me. The expression on her face was of undisguised relish. I found that, for all the assumed casualness of my pausing there, I was tense and shivering in the heat. I composed my voice, and said to Muriel, "I'll just go down and see how they're getting on."

I was careful to make a great noise as I descended the ladder. "Hullo," Tony said, "You come to watch?"

"Yes."

"Well, there's not much to see."

I sat down. The air was hot and close. "Go on. Give me a demonstration," I said.

"I'm not trying to lift anything heavy, y'see. Not got the strength for it nowadays really, and they say you mustn't overstrain. I just do press-ups and that."

"You could do those on deck where it's cooler."

"Suppose so. But we're used to it down here, aren't we, Sonn?"

"Are you?" I said to Sonya.

Tony said, "Go on, Sonn. You show him some of your stuff. Squats and stuff."

"Pliés." Sonya was embarrassed, and, I could see, angry, though without yet quite knowing why. She said, "I can't do them before——"

"Strangers?"

"Anyone. I don't like practising in public. It makes me shy. Anyway, there's nothing to see."

The two of them stood there awkwardly, gazing at me. Something was wrong. I had interrupted; I was indeed a stranger. I had brought the musky stench of the tigers with me into the hold, and the atmosphere had become oppressive.

"We're finished anyway," Sonya said. "It's too hot down here to do much," and the two of them climbed back up the ladder to the deck, and left me sitting there alone.

Gertrude said, "I'll tell you something. I was not a great actress. Good, but not great. Perhaps I was too intelligent."

As tar breaks out in bubbles upon the roads during hot weather, our secret thoughts began to come out of us as we lay there in the sun. "I began to have doubts, you see," Gertrude said.

"You did?"

"Yes. Isn't that strange? Not very often at first. Just sometimes at night. Perhaps if people didn't sleep alone . . . but I never married; nobody lasted long enough with me. Sir Charles Cochran once told me I was too intense for life—born for the theatre, not for life, he said. But then, he had to be polite because he was turning me down for a job."

"What doubts?" I said.

"Whether it was all worth while."

"Casting couch and that?"

"Not that so much. Surprisingly little of that goes on, though people like to think so. One finds it more on the variety stage, with agents of the shadier sort, and sometimes the smallest parts . . . or ASM's. . . . But really, my dear, people are far more ready to offer than directors are to accept. There is so much competition, and so little talent. Boys from the Midlands who've been playing at being artistic all their lives, and don't want to go into the family business. And the girls—once they used to visit the sick, but nowadays it's the stage—something to do with the need for self-expression, but why the public should suffer it, I never could tell. And all those silly irresponsible people one found; I suppose it's because professionals have a reputation for irresponsibility that so many irresponsible people think they ought to enter the profession. But it won't do. My dear, there always used to be such a fuss because eighty per cent of us were unemployed, but they never considered how many of us were unemployable."

"But your doubts."

"They grew deeper. First of all, I doubted the value of the theatre as I knew it."

"As we all knew it," I said.

Banner said, "I never knew it. Except for the amateurs, of course. We used to write away to the British Drama League for one-act plays with an all-female cast."

"Most of us were discontented with the theatre," Gertrude said. "There were articles about that every Sunday. Once television came along, you could hardly get the public to go to anything if there wasn't a cash prize in it somewhere. Then there were the costs, and rents going up and all that, and people worked it out that you had to run for a year or you weren't making a profit, or something; I could never understand it. I played Antigone in the West End when I was twenty-four. Six years ago, I went back to the same theatre, but this time I was playing the mother-in-law in a kitchen comedy. I was so full of life when I was young. I had written "Gertrude Harrison. Actress" in pencil on the wall by my dressing-table, and it was still there when I went back, so I crossed out the "Actress". . . . During our second year in that play, people came by charabanc from Widnes to see us. They never did that for Antigone."

"But Goodness!" I said. "If that was all that bothered you——"

"No, of course not. Those who loved the theatre only did so more strongly when there was less of it. The Third Programme revived my Antigone, and there was the High-brow Theatre Club. Do you remember?—it gave you a kind of joint membership of the Arts, the Royal Court, the Mermaid, and the Comedy, and there was some kind of income tax deduction if you bought more than ten tickets in a year. Whenever we lost one theatre, another smaller one took its place, like the Shakespeare group in Southwark who converted an old stable into an Elizabethan playhouse after the Old Vic had been taken over by the Secondary Schools Association."

"I remember," I said. "Publishers used to advertise in the programmes, and *Encounter* was on sale in the foyers. Still, it all helped to keep the theatre alive."

"My dear, that was the trouble; I kept wondering why. Don't you see?—my doubts weren't concerned with what was happening to the theatre, but with the nature of the theatrical experience itself. It was my religion; it always had been. Beauty, art, all the highest things—they really took the place of God for me. I believed so strongly in them, until I began to lie awake at night, wondering what was high and what was low, and whether one was any better than the other, and whether I just used 'high' and 'low' without thinking, and whether everybody else did the same. And then I began to think about theatrical values— You know that thrill up the spine one used to get whenever one was in the presence of what we called 'real theatre'?"

"Yes, I think so."

"I discovered it could be *self-induced*. And I began to wonder whether the whole thing wasn't just a daydream we had made up for ourselves to prove we were people of greater sensibility. The whole thing. Everything that had given meaning to my life. Everything I was trying to teach my pupils. Of course, I didn't give in without a struggle. I read all I could about aesthetics. I went back to my Jung and my Plato—books I'd been given, you know, when I was younger (for I'd been a great success among academic people, and always preferred them to the businessmen). . . . They were books I hadn't opened much, but I went through them all . . . Myths . . . Ritual . . . The nature of tragedy . . . Catharsis . . . I could come away from a performance of *Lear* feeling noble and ⸀ uplifted, I knew, but I also found I could get the same feeling from benzedrine."

"But surely," Banner said, "it is not only a matter of experience. One learns from great plays, does one not?"

"What?" I said.

"About the nature of life."

I said, "I should have thought you'd learn more about the nature of life from one week as a social worker than from ten years of steady theatre-going. Isn't that so, Gertrude?"

Banner interrupted. "But Gertrude, how could you teach if you felt like this?" he said.

"I didn't have doubts all the time, you know. When I did, I would go to bed until I felt better. Doubts are only intermittent; otherwise they would be certainties. Oh, I would forget for a while, and go on in the old way, and it would be quite genuine. I didn't pretend. Did you think I was pretending when we had our readings, or I recited to you?"

"No, I didn't."

"What I have felt at the moment, I have always felt completely. I used to think that a virtue; it is a very essential quality for us in the profession; I would always tell my pupils so." Gertrude sighed. "But during the last few days, as my doubts have been coming back, they have forced me to look at the whole of my life, all the moments added together, and they amount to so very little." We were all silent for a while. "It's very strange," Gertrude said, "Arthur told me. . . . He sees these things so differently. He told me there would be a place—that I should look upon it not as an end in itself, but as a skill. . . . He said that what I have been doing all my life is not wrong—because, you know, when my doubts were on me, I thought it was very wrong. . . . It is a matter of proportion, he said."

"Of control."

"What?"

"Of control," Banner said. "It is all a matter of control; Arthur has assured me of that. Now we are to start again, he says. Things had got out of hand. That is why I was able to do no good. I had my own doubts, you know. I think all of us do."

"You too? But if you never had a vocation in the first place, why were you bothered by doubts?" I said.

"Not of a religious nature. Of a practical nature. Christianity was not important to me, as you know. Perhaps it should have been, but you either have that sort of faith, or you haven't. The faith I had was that I could help people, and the doubts I had were that my help wasn't doing any good. It was all so complex. One tried to work on simple premises. Justice and injustice . . . it wasn't as easy as that. For instance, I discovered—I was bound to when so many of my parishioners were in and out of prison—that the police often *invent* evidence. That made me very angry at first."

"Are you sure of this?"

"Quite sure. After all, it's fairly well known among the legal people, and cases got into the papers from time to time, you know, and sometimes an unfortunate policeman would be sent to prison himself."

"Unfortunate!"

"Yes. Because one sees their point of view as well. The police do not look upon the safeguards of the law as we do, you see, but as restrictions to be circumvented. Very often they know that some unhappy man has committed a crime, and they would feel—well, foolish if he were to escape conviction by some technicalities of the evidence. Of course they begin with an advantage. Most juries and all magistrates attach much more weight to the evidence of a police officer than they do to that of an ordinary witness. Juries very seldom realize, you see, that the police are interested parties, and that it is a point of pride of the police to get a conviction. I was very angry when I first discovered this, because the police are only human, and they do make mistakes. When they have come to a conclusion, they do not easily reverse it, so that there are cases when they have decided that someone is guilty when he is in fact quite innocent, and, in pinning the crime on him, the police commit an injustice. I found that very difficult to stomach, until it was pointed out to me that the alternative to this procedure would allow so many criminals to escape that the civilized society I valued would itself be imperilled. After a while I accepted this view, but it was not an easy one to explain to those who had themselves suffered under the system— I could accept it logically, if you like, that it was sometimes necessary for the police to place dust from the scene of a robbery in the trouser turn-ups of the spare suit of the man whom they believed to have committed it, but I could not accept it emotionally. Eventually I became very mixed up in my mind."

Gertrude said, "But your work? This one thing was not enough to make you doubt the whole value of that?"

"No, but there were similar complications about so many things. Youth Clubs. They were such a good work. We needed them to keep young people off the streets, and to bring friends to lonely people. But in order to attract the youngsters into coming, and staying, I had to use what methods I could. I found that in one case

all I had done was to create the nucleus of a gang; they
wrecked the Club, and I had to disband it. Then on
the advice of a colleague, I went in for evening classes
and scenes from Shakespeare, but that didn't take, so
we fell back on table tennis. Then there were the undesirables. I could not be present the whole time; they
would not have liked that. You would say I should have
got rid of the undesirables, but they were the people
who most needed help. . . . There were so many things.
Nothing I did turned out simply well, and more and
more I came to doubt whether I myself knew what was
best. That is where a vocation might have helped me;
at least I could have worked to rule. Finally came the
deepest doubt of all. I began to doubt my own motives.
It was something I overheard—a man talking about me
in anger. He said I was bossy, and, you know, I realized
that he was right. All my social purpose—just bossiness
and wanting to tell people what to do. Like Gertrude,
I had to go on. That was my job, and I was in the middle
of too many things. I had to live in the moment, and
hope that I was right. But the doubts would always be
waiting for me when I was tired or things were turning
out badly."

"Mice," said Gertrude. "Eating away at the rim of
the mind."

"If you like. But there will be no mice when the
waters subside; the animals have not, if you will allow
the joke, come in two by two. Our numbers are small
enough to control. We can make a good start this time."

I said, "Whatever sort of start we make, we shan't be
alive to know whether it was good or not when the results
come in."

"Arthur will see to it."

"Yes," Banner said, "Arthur will see to the results. We
only have to do what is right."

"And how shall we know?"

"Arthur will tell us."

"But good God," I said. "How can Arthur or anyone else possibly know——?"

"Arthur will do it." Banner was angry and earnest. "I will not have this sort of speculation. It will all be controlled from the beginning."

"Of course," Gertrude said, "it is a matter of proportion."

"A murderer!" I said. There was an immediate silence. "Arthur's our leader, and we depend on him, but he's not God," I said. "He's not above doing foolish and wicked things; you know that. It wouldn't have hurt us to take in that man from the ark, but Arthur murdered him."

"How hot it is!" Banner said. "We must be careful not to get too excited."

Gertrude said, "I remember that as a very *little* girl, I could lie all day in the sun. I used to soak it up. Mother said I was storing up energy for the winter."

My eyes filled with tears. "You don't want to hear," I said. "You just lie here airing your bloody doubts, but you won't allow yourself to think about— You won't listen. You're afraid of being upset."

"But we are not afraid of anything," Gertrude said. "Not while Arthur is here to look after us."

That night I found it more than usually difficult to sleep. Whom could I trust? Sonya?—whether I could or not was out of the question, for obviously I did not. Tony?—he was an aching spot in my mind; I could not even directly hate him, since, whatever he and Sonya might have done together, he would not have taken the lead. Gertrude? Banner? Muriel?—they were Arthur's creatures, and Arthur was mad, a figure from a horror comic. They were all mad, I thought, all mad but I, the single sane being in this small mad world. *Mad, bad,* the jingle went round in my mind, and *dangerous to know,* dangerous to me, dangerous to themselves, to each other, to Sonya, to me, to me. . . .

The other men in the cabin were sleeping; I could hear them breathing in counterpoint. But something moved. Someone came out of the women's room. A figure, moving swiftly on bare feet, passed by us, and went out on deck. I saw her framed in the open door only for the fraction of a moment, and it was not long enough for me to be able to tell who she was. Soon, I thought, someone from our own room would follow her. Soon Tony would get up and follow her, and I should know for certain.

There was a shuffling sound in the darkness. He was getting up, slowly and carefully. He was pausing for a moment beside each sleeper, listening to their breathing to make sure they were asleep. I closed my eyes, and moaned as if in a dream, and he went quickly by me. As he opened the door, I saw that he was not Tony, but Arthur.

I forced myself to wait before following him out on deck, for I dared not seem to be spying. I must not move stealthily. If I were discovered, it must appear that I had come out in all innocence to breathe the night air. I pushed open the door casually, and stepped out. I could see nobody outside, but dared not peer about me. I walked a little way towards the edge of the raft, and looked at the phosphorescence in the water. There was nobody on deck, unless they were hidden in the shadows of the other side of the cabin, but I could not go to see. There was nothing for me to do but wait a while, and then go back indoors.

"Not now," a voice said. "Make your report first." It was Arthur's voice, and it was faint and far below me. I turned quickly, and glared into the darkness. Was Arthur a ventriloquist, sending his voice out to plague me while he himself sniggered in the shadows? Then, as Muriel answered, I realized that the voices came from the hold, and silently I took up my station at the top of the ladder to eavesdrop.

"Make your report."

Muriel said, "They're carrying on."

"Who are?"

"Miss Banks and Mr. Ryle."

"Have you seen them?"

It seemed to me that a long time passed between the question and Muriel's answer to it. A hunger for and fear of the truth grew together in my mind. Then Muriel said, "No, but he knows."

"How can you tell?"

"I've been watching him. He can't keep his mind off it when they're down here together. And she knows he knows. She's been giving him some very funny looks."

"And Mr. Ryle?"

"You can't tell what that kind are thinking about. But it stands to reason, doesn't it?"

There was a pause. Then Muriel's voice again, eager and complicit. "Arthur?"

"Yes."

"What are you going to do about it?"

"Nothing."

"But they're carrying on."

"It is suitable that they should. Miss Banks is more realistic than her—than Mr. Clarke. She knows that when we have settled down, such mattters will have to be arranged on a more rational basis than they are at present. She is unlikely to object therefore to being, as it were, shared. Should she do so, it will be enough to confront her with what we already know; that she has been promiscuous for her pleasure, and may be expected to continue to be promiscuous for the profit of the community as a whole."

"Shared?"

A silence.

"Shall I be shared, Arthur?"

"Of course."

Muriel giggled; it was a little horrible to hear her. "Well, it'll make a change," she said.

Arthur said, "What else have you to tell me?"

"He's been talking against you."

"Who?"

"Mr. Clarke."

"In what way?"

"He said you were a murderer. He said that to Harold and Gertrude this afternoon. He said you did foolish and wicked things."

"Foolish?"

"That's what he said."

"And what did they reply?"

"They said it was very hot."

"Foolish!" Arthur said, "I should be angry if I did not consider the source. Let Mr. Clarke be a warning to you, Muriel. He has intelligence, but no wisdom."

"Aren't you going to punish him?"

"No."

"Not when he's been talking against you?"

"It is of no consequence; he does no harm. Mr. Clarke is without a backbone, my dear. He may destroy himself with doubts and scruples, hesitations and evasions, but he cannot destroy us because, when it comes to the point, he will always do what he is told. Meanwhile he is an excellent cook."

A silence again. Muriel said, "There's nothing else, Arthur?"

"Nothing?"

"Unless. . . . Unless you wanted anything, Arthur."

"You must not be coy, my dear," Arthur said. "It is not becoming in a widow of your years." They did not speak much after that, and I did not feel inclined to eavesdrop any longer. I went back to my pallet, and lay down, and before Arthur returned, I was asleep.

I had said, "We're never alone together nowadays," and it was true. Now when at last I had decided to "have it out" with Sonya, there was nowhere I could be sure of privacy. I could not say, "Come down into the hold," the suggestion carried too many sickening associations, and besides I knew Muriel would be watching us.

I tried to begin the conversation many times, but I was always held back by the fear that we should be discovered in a "scene", and everyone would know. In any case, I kept reminding myself, taxing Sonya with her infidelity would change nothing, although I knew in fact that something had already been changed; suspicion had been changed to certainty. I have heard it said that hope is only a torment to a man, who without it might adapt himself to necessity. Things were not so consolingly arranged for me. Hope and fear had battled together in my mind, and now that the battle was over, the Occupation had begun, and it was worse than the battle.

In the end it was Sonya who "had it out" with me. "What's the matter with you nowadays?" she said. "You're always looking at me in a funny way. It makes me nervous."

It was astonishingly difficult to tell her what the matter was. I began with Muriel's report. Sonya listened in silence, and then said, "And you believe her?"

I said, "You said yourself——"

"What did I say?"

"You said, 'It's only sex'. You said it as if . . . as if sex wasn't important to you. As if it was something you could have with anyone."

"What *is* important then?" Sonya said.

I could not answer. Sonya's face bore a sulky obstinate expression. "Well," she said, "if you've made up your mind, there's nothing more to be done, is there?"

I said, "Sonya, is it true?"

"You don't know, do you?"

"I want to know."

"You can't expect me to tell you."

I wanted to strike her. I wanted to seize and shake her. I wanted to smash and hurt both Sonya and myself, to wipe out the whole thing in a blaze of pain and violence. But I could do none of these things. I could only stare at her, and she stared back at me, while the sun shone down outside, and the raft lay still in the ocean, and it seemed as if we were trapped in a moment that would never end.

"Anyway, I'll tell you one thing," Sonya said, "I've been saving it up to tell you for a week now. It's funny really. I'm going to have a baby."

I said, "Sonya!"

"I thought you'd be pleased."

"I am. Sonya darling, I am."

"Are you?" she said. "Well, that won't last long, will it? After all, you don't know whose it is."

9. Trial and Error

It was two months since the tempest. We had spent the time in doubt and idleness, with little to eat and less to drink.

As we began to feel the effects of Arthur's "water discipline," our physical condition deteriorated alarmingly. We were not pretty people. Under the sunburn, our skins had become swollen, puffy and tender to the touch. Our eyes had receded; it was as if someone had amused himself by pushing holes with his thumb in the swollen flesh of our faces. Our lips were cracked and stiff, and the cheeks and throats of the men were covered with an itching stubble. Our tongues had begun to swell and in swelling were pushed forward so that the tips protruded from our mouths; when we spoke, we slurred and stumbled in our speech like morons. We were saved from scurvy by the vitamin C in our moistened Glub, but the evening slop of raw fish induced in us all a running flux, and added humiliation to weakness. Most of the time, during these last days, we lay about on deck. We had lost our dignity and our self-respect, and so much of our humanity. We were animals indeed, but not the rational animals of Arthur's vision.

The arrow on the dial of the ammeter fell back and back. Arthur told us that we should have to row. We had done it before, he reminded us, when we had towed the raft to the old man's ark. Now we were to propel the raft through the water to charge the batteries.

I remember that experience as a sort of after-image. If one closes one's eyes very tightly against the light, what one sees first of all is just redness; then the after-

images begin to form, making pictures and patterns that
are always changing, sometimes suddenly and sometimes
by degrees, as when a line of telegraph poles turned into
centipedes diagonally from the bottom right hand corner.
It is a memory like that. First of all, only a redness, and
then streaks and white-hot rain and zigzags in the redness,
and then pictures, which are for the most part of faces,
distorted in close-up. Muriel, her tongue like pink bubble
gum, her hair matted and disordered, straining her full
weight against an oar that did not move. Banner, rowing
and feathering, rowing and feathering meticulously some
six inches above the surface of the water. Hunter's enormous vacancy above a nest of beard. A pair of hands
with the skin scraped off the palms. Muriel again, face
upwards in the dinghy, her lips drawn back over her
gums in a snarl. No picture for Arthur, but only a thin
persistent cawing, a single syllable that he meant for
"Row!", but his obstructing tongue would not allow him
to make an "R", and his dry throat turned the rest to
croaking.

With the pictures, fears and sensations. How long?
How long must I? How long can I? A fear for Sonya
and for what this might do to the child, young as it
still was in her womb—*they jump off tables, don't they,
to stop it?* Pain. The pain of not being able to sweat.
Surprise that, when Arthur gave us water to sustain us,
it seemed to break out at once in drops all over the skin,
but the drops dried, and our throats were dry again, and
our tongues were weighted stockings, dragging us down
to the bottom of the dinghy. Then complete, wonderful,
healing exhaustion, the giving in utterly, the knowing
that we could do no more, that Arthur had driven us to
the furthest limits of our strength, and it was not enough.

I do not remember now whether, after all that pain
and effort, we moved the raft at all. Certainly, if we did,
the benefit to the batteries was more than cancelled by
Arthur's having to dole out extra water to keep us going,
and more water still to entice us out of the dinghy and

back on board again. The endeavour had failed, as it was bound to fail, and he would have to think of something else, while we continued to endure.

Dying of thirst is something to do with the amount of water in the blood. Ninety per cent of one's blood plasma is water, and when this percentage is decreased, one's blood gets thicker, and the chemistry of the cells is upset so that they can no longer function. After our attempt to charge the batteries of the raft by towing it, we had reached a physical state in which it seemed to me that we should die quite soon, so I went to Arthur to tell him so. That was the one intelligent thing that I did at this time, and I remember it with all the more pleasure, because this wise deed was followed shortly afterwards by some very foolish words.

Arthur was sitting in the cabin, the journal open in front of him as usual. But he seemed to have no heart or strength to write in it, and just sat there, staring into the future. I took the book and the ball-point pen that lay beside it, and wrote on a blank page, "If we do not get water, we shall die."

Arthur opened his mouth to reply, but the words dried on his tongue. Then he took the book and pen from me, and wrote, "Need to ration."

I wrote, "Ration not sufficient."

Arthur wrote, "Must make it last."

I wrote, "Deterioration gets faster. Medical fact. If Natural Selection in earnest, surely water will be provided."

Arthur wrote, "Yes." Then he went to the cooler, and gave me a drink, and took a drink for himself, and then we took water to the others. Arthur said that we must go carefully, but that we might finish what was in the cooler on that day, and we should distil another lot in the evening.

It was very strange after so long to be able to drink enough. A glass of water, when one has been without it for a long time, is not a taste but a sensation. One does not drink the water; one absorbs it as the dry earth absorbs rain, which seems to soak instantly into every cell and fibre. So first of all we absorbed the water and then, out of luxury, we drank some, and before we could drink too much and prove the old travellers' tales all over again, we had exhausted the contents of the cooler. Thereafter there was nothing to do but to go to sleep until Arthur roused us to prepare the evening meal, and when we had eaten it, we went to sleep again.

Next morning, Arthur said, "As Mr. Clarke has reminded me, Natural Selection cannot reasonably intend us to perish. We must find some way of raising a wind."

Hunter said, "Whistle for one. I tried it once in the Pacific."

"Did it work?"

"No. Could have been my own fault, though. Not a good whistler."

"Superstition," Arthur said.

Muriel said, "Arthur doesn't care for superstition. You know that."

Arthur looked at me. "You are in some sense responsible, Mr. Clarke," he said. "It was you who aroused me from—ah, that sweet way I was in to despair. Perhaps, when you did so, you had some sort of plan?"

"I'm sorry, Arthur. I'm afraid I didn't."

"Do you care for superstition, Mr. Clarke?"

I said, "Primitive people——"

"Yes, we must be primitive certainly. What do primitive people do in these circumstances? Tell us, Mr. Clarke."

"They—they go in for magic a lot. They throw coins into the sea, or nail a gold piece to the mast, or something like that."

"Perhaps you have a gold piece with you?"

"No."

"Then we must begin with coins."

Muriel was found to have a small purse of black silk. It contained nine and sevenpence in cash and two pound notes. Arthur threw the nine and sevenpence into the sea, coin by coin. We watched them turning over and over in the clear water until they disappeared. Then Arthur wadded up the pound notes into pellets, and dropped them also into the sea. One of them was almost immediately eaten by a fish. "The gift has been accepted," Arthur said.

But there was no wind. We sat on the edge of the deck and whistled, but there was no wind. First we whistled tunes, and then we whistled wind noises, but there was no wind. We blew with our mouths, but there was no wind, and we beat a wet rag against the cold iron of the stove, but there was no wind. In the afternoon, we brought out a tub, and filled it with seawater, and we slooshed the water about from side to side of the tub to make waves in sympathetic magic, but the waves were not sympathetic enough, and there was no wind.

"Have you any other suggestions, Mr. Clarke?" Arthur asked.

"Not unless you have anyone in mind for Iphigenia." In the silence that followed, Gertrude looked directly at me, and I could see that she was frightened. I began to blush, and, since the flippancy could not be unsaid, made matters worse by qualifying it. "Wouldn't be any good anyway," I said. "You're not a father, Arthur, and we couldn't even get by with a virgin, because there isn't one on board."

Arthur had not taken the reference. He said, "I do not understand you."

Banner said, "Iphigenia——" and then he too caught Gertrude's glance, and stopped.

I said quickly, "What did the Ancient Mariner do?"

"The two cases are not on a level. We have nothing to expiate." As Arthur stood in thought, I realized that once the process of looking for literary parallels had begun, there was no stopping it. "Jonah, however. . . ." Arthur said. "Although the problem there was not to cause a storm, but to stop one."

For some time Tony, who usually said nothing during a discussion, had been struggling with a thought. "I don't know about this magic and stuff," he said, "I thought—I mean there is something. When I was a kid at school, I burned a spot in me wrist with the sun."

Sonya said, "Of course. A burning glass."

"To raise a wind?"

"No, but we could use it to distil water. We can't use the wind to power the batteries, because there isn't any wind, but we only want the power for heat, and we can get that from the sun."

Tony said, "There's lots of packing cases and stuff downstairs. I thought we could make a fire or something."

Banner said, "Why use wood at all? Why not a direct beam?"

Gertrude said, "Oh, my dear Tony, what a good idea! You have saved us all. Under Arthur's direction of course," and Muriel, glancing quickly at Arthur to make sure that he approved, echoed her, "A good idea, Tony."

It seemed to me, however, that Arthur was not entirely pleased. Jealous people are sensitive to the jealousies of others, and I detected in Arthur some of the sour envy that I felt within myself. It was really too simple an idea; if we had thought of it sooner, all of us would have been saved so much suffering. It must have been very humiliating for Arthur that a solution should come from somebody whose intelligence he despised; besides, that was not Tony's function in the new society. For the present, he did no more than to order Hunter to find or make a magnifying glass, and he withdrew into the cabin, asking Gertrude to go with him. "I did not understand what Mr. Clarke meant by Iphigenia, my dear," he said. "You must explan that to me."

"Silly cow!" Muriel said, and went to sit outside the cabin, just beneath the window where she could eavesdrop easily.

It was not possible in fact to make a burning glass,

for we had nothing like the rotating metal disc with which glass is ground. Nor could Hunter find a magnifying glass anywhere on board, so, after experimenting with the bottom of a bottle, we settled for the curved metal shaving mirror in the bathroom. Although the beam we got from it was not strong enough to boil a flask of water, it would certainly start a fire. For fuel there were the crates in the hold, and Glub Cushions, we found, burned slowly like charcoal if we did not use too many at a time and damped them a little with brine first. Should it ever become necessary, we could burn part of the cabin; my imagination played with the idea of using the raft itself, burning it day by day in pieces until only a tiny square was left, just sufficient to hold the fireplace. In any event, we had enough fuel to be able to distil a generous water ration, and to ensure that our evening stew need no longer be eaten raw. Our tongues moved easily in our mouths now, and the distress of our bodies was much abated. You might think that the situation had returned to what it was before, but you would be wrong. There was a change.

At first, as if to compensate for our previous lethargy, we were as active as we could be. We constructed a hearth on the deck of the raft, and set a grate above it. We broke up packing cases, and stacked the pieces in a pile. We brought the cooking implements out on deck, and arranged them in what was now our new kitchen. While Arthur wrote and wrote in the journal, the rest of us cleaned and prepared the fish for supper, and Gertrude went down on her knees afterwards to scrub the deck. We were like children playing at house.

Then that passed, for really there was not enough to do, but the feeling of being in a children's world persisted. Hunter, our fisherman, sat in his usual place at the edge of the raft, racked by giggles, and said it was because he was thinking of Words. Banner and Gertrude cornered Tony, and whiled away an hour or so by asking him easy riddles and questions on general knowledge.

"You're very clever, Tony," Gertrude said in admiration after he had answered three in succession correctly, and Tony, thinking he was being baited, turned sulky and refused to play any longer.

Then Banner did a malicious thing. On the second morning of this new period, Gertrude rose early; she thought that she might come across another seal. Indeed there was one, she said, at the end of the raft, but it was frightened by the sudden opening of the door, and fled at once into the water. Gertrude decided to follow it. She undressed, and dived into the sea, puffing, and splashing, and blowing the water in little fountains from her mouth in the hope that the seal would return and sport with her, but it would not. Meanwhile Banner came out on deck, saw her in the water, laughed, and took away her clothes. Gertrude did not wish to appear before us naked, but after some time she became tired. Then she discovered that she was not strong enough to pull herself back on deck. She called out, but there was nobody to hear her except Banner, who returned and said, "What if there should be sharks as well as seals?" Then he helped her out of the water, and Gertrude tried to dry herself on her bikini with one hand, and cover herself with the other.

Gertrude complained to Arthur, who reprimanded Banner and ordered him to apologize. For the rest of that day, Gertrude and Banner would not speak to one another, except that Banner announced that if he could catch a seal, he would kill it and eat it. Gertrude said, "You're not to. You're not to," but Banner replied that it would be doing the seal a kindness, because, not being guided as we were guided, the seal was bound to go wrong and suffer. "They never know," he said. "They never know what will happen, or what people will think, or anything. Death is the only certainty for such creatures. There is great certainty in death," and Gertrude said, "I'll death you if you touch my seals," and there the matter rested.

Sonya stacked the plates, and took them away into the galley. "I want to make my position clear," Arthur said. We sat up straight in our seats, folded our hands in our laps, and gave him our attention. In rummaging through the contents of the hold for fuel, we had come across a crate of candles, and one of these stood in a saucer at the head of the table, its flame a steady yellow tear-drop of light, burning upwards in the still air.

"It is the mark of the rational man," Arthur said, "that he is prepared to change his mind. The man who never changes his mind is the man who has ceased thinking. I despise such a man." At once I felt myself to be the man who never changed his mind and was despised by Arthur. Banner coughed and moved uneasily in his seat. The rest were silent. Arthur said, "An attitude to life and to the problems of human society can be no more than a hypothesis. As more facts are discovered, the hypothesis is modified. Perhaps it is discarded altogether in favour of another hypothesis. I hope everyone here will agree with me."

The silence continued. Finally I said, "Yes, Arthur."

Arthur said, "I have been thinking about the value of myth. We are, after all, in a mythological situation. Our descendants will remember us, not simply as the haphazard survivors of a great catastrophe, but as the founders, the chosen, the people who came out of the sea to beget a new race. Indeed, why should they not do so, for that is what we are?"

"Yes, Arthur."

"For their own self-respect as a people, they must remember us as greater than we are. From our loins they will all spring." (How impossible it was to think of Arthur as having loins!) "We should not wonder then that they may build a little on the facts, that future playwrights and people of the theatre, for instance, should identify their craft with Miss Harrison's interest in it, that men of muscle should remember Mr. Ryle, that cooks should light a candle to Mr. Clarke. They may remember me as the leader of you all, as the source of all power, all benefits. They may do that. We know, of course, that we are not gods and goddesses, but human beings—although beings specially marked out by Natural Selection for survival—but it may be for the benefit of our descendants that *they* should believe so."

None of the gods and goddesses at the table had the grace to blush. I said, "I'd rather be the god of copywriting than of cookery, Arthur, if it's all the same to you."

Arthur said, "Now let me approach our situation from another angle. As I see it, the parlour magic with which we have so far experimented cannot be expected to work, because we do not ourselves believe in it. We do not even behave as if we did so. It is, as it were, out of context. We have tried to take over one part of the pattern of life that pertains to a primitive people, while discarding the rest. But if there should be any supernatural forces at all, they do not exist permissively, but pervade the fabric, dictate indeed the circumstances of our everyday life."

We were all of us listening with close attention; Hunter, Tony, Muriel and Sonya because, in their own varying degrees, they were not sure what Arthur was talking about; Gertrude and Banner because they were following the course of his argument; myself because I was trying to anticipate it. Arthur wiped his spectacles. "So then," he said, "we have two situations, very different in kind, both of which, however, lead us to the same way of behaving. On the one hand we have a duty to our descendants to behave in a manner appropriate to the myth in which we are participants. On the other, if we are to solve our immediate difficulties and succeed in raising a wind by supernatural means, we must live in such a way that, if I may allow myself a play on words, the supernatural can come naturally."

Nobody laughed.

"What makes a god?" Arthur said. "Any thinking person will tell you that men make their own gods. They do so by worship. Whatever you worship is God, whether it be a tree, or the sun, or two sticks, or a ring of stones, or a bull, or a lamb, or a river; it does not matter. Simple men worship the things themselves. Complicated men worship the ideas that the things express, or the spirit that infuses the things, but in terms of behaviour it makes very little difference. The behaviour—the ritual, if you prefer—is what matters, because, while interpretations change, the ritual endures. Is that not so, Mr. Banner?"

"Very largely, Arthur."

"Very largely?"

"Entirely."

"Good. It is a problem, then, of behaviour. First, if we wish to raise a wind by magic, we must behave as if we believed in magic, and after a while perhaps we shall believe. Secondly, if we wish our descendants to maintain those high principles with which we ourselves are inspired, we must behave as if those principles had a more than human inspiration." Arthur looked steadily round the table, his gaze reaching into the shadows cast by the candle flame, and fixing each of us in turn. "You had better begin by worshippping me," he said. "Some of you may feel at first that I am unworthy of the honour. You must conquer that feeling. It will in any case die with you, while what is recorded of your behaviour will live on as revealed religion. Are there any questions?"

There were no questions.

"Very well," Arthur said, "Mr. Banner, will you give thanks?"

Banner looked up timidly, and Arthur gave him an encouraging nod. "For what we have just received," Banner said, "may Arthur make us truly thankful."

"That's right," Arthur said, "and so I do."

10. The Two Currents

Tony said he could see fog on the horizon. Fog or smoke.

I said, "A forest fire perhaps?"

"Well, you know. It could be a ship burning or something. I mean, we burned——"

"What did we burn, Mr. Ryle?" Arthur had come out of the cabin to join us.

Tony was embarrassed. "I don't want to quarrel with anyone," he said, "I mean, you knew what you were doing, I don't deny."

"Then do not be led into the sort of remarks in which you might be tempted to deny it. It is unlike you. I fear you have been thinking too much lately. We are all grateful to you for that, of course, but if you allow it to become a habit, it may upset you. Why not tell us exactly what you have seen, if you can put it into words, and leave us to speculate about how it came there?"

I said, "I'll take a look. It's probably only heat haze."

"Oh, for Christ's sake, stop getting at Tony all the time," Sonya said, "I'm sick of hearing you."

"Miss Banks?"

"I'm sorry, Arthur. I don't mean you. You've got a right to pick on us if you want to. But I'm tired of the way——"

Tony said, "That's all right, Sonn."

My throat was dry, and I felt humiliatingly close to tears. I said, "Why don't you— You're ready enough to pick on me." Dislike and envy of Tony combined with a conviction of being treated unfairly to make a pale feeling of unease in my bladder. I moved away, and stared out to sea.

"Bloody childish," Sonya said.

"What do you see, Mr. Clarke?"

I could see fog. The sun was shining in my eyes, so that it was difficult to get a clear view, but it seemed to me that the distant horizon had lost its curve, and a straight grey wall cut the rim of the world. "It's a long way away," I said, "I don't know if it'll get any closer."

But it did get closer. Slowly the grey wall spread and spread. It gained height and width and the impression of depth. All of us were gathered on deck, staring in the one direction as the long hours passed and the fog wall grew in size. "I do not understand what impels it," Arthur said. "If there were a wind, surely we should feel some motion of it in our sails. And the fog moves so slowly."

Banner said, "I suppose . . . I suppose we may not be moving towards *it*? Drift . . . sea-drift. . . . The edge of the world was said to be a place of fogs."

I saw Muriel turn the whites of her eyes towards him like a frightened animal. Arthur said, "The world is round."

"Yes."

Gertrude said, "It is like. . . . It is a little like *Outward Bound*. When one makes the crossing between this world and the next. . . ."

Sonya said, "I saw a picture once about the Niagara Falls. They were all steamy. Marilyn Monroe was in it."

"How could we be moving? We have been becalmed. We still are."

"Yes."

I said, "It's not another tidal wave at any rate; we can be thankful for that. It's only fog. It won't do us any harm."

"Where does it come from?"

Muriel said, "I wish we'd never come. I wish we'd stayed at home. Once we. . . . We don't know how thick it is, or anything."

Banner said, "After the sun—mist".

"Well, it'll make a change anyway," Tony said.

Slowly, slowly we drew nearer. The horizon had long since disappeared. We had thought at first that we could see above the wall—that is, that we could see a top to the fog, above which there was clear sky—but now the fog reached up, infecting the sky with its own greyness.

A tiny wave chopped sideways at the raft. "This is ridiculous," Arthur said. "There is no wind to inspire rough water."

"Look! What's happened to the sea?"

Stretching towards us over the surface of the water, extending for perhaps a mile from the bank of fog, there was a brown discolouration. "It's poisonous," Gertrude whispered. "It poisons the water."

"Nonsense," Arthur said, "it is only weed."

"We've never seen weed before."

"We see it now."

We drew closer. The weed did not lie on the water as an unbroken layer; this was not the Sargasso Sea of the boys' adventure stories. Nor was it motionless. It was splashed and scattered about as if it had been thrown there, and it seemed to drift steadily, as we were now unmistakeably drifting, towards the wall of fog, there to be caught in some sort of eddy, repelled, and thrown out again. "It seems," Arthur said, "that we are in a current." All this time we had been drifting with an enormous body of water, and, having nothing to measure our progress by, had imagined ourselves to be in the same place. We had been motionless, sure enough, but the water in which we lay had a motion of its own.

The grey wall did not immediately envelop us when we entered it; instead, the experience was as ordinary as walking into low cloud among mountains. First there was the clear air, then an area that was part mist, and then all mist, each stage passing easily into the next. We had fallen silent, and drew a little closer to one another. Suddenly Banner sneezed. "Gesundheit," I said mechanically. "Thank you," said Banner. The mist was chilly and damp. "Are we adequately clad for this climate,

I wonder," Arthur said. "Surely we had more clothing when we came aboard?"

"Your oilskins, Arthur?"

"No. Blankets."

The women scurried into the cabin for blankets. "We look like a lot of Red Indians, I must say," Sonya said, after we had wrapped them around our shoulders.

Now we were in the midst of the fog, and could not see even to the other edge of the raft. Behind us there was a sudden flopping sound as something hit the deck. Gertrude sat next to me, and I could feel her jump. Arthur said, "Go and see what it is," and Hunter padded off in the direction of the sound. When he returned, he was carrying a fish. "Jumped right out of the water," he said. "Silly little bastard must have lost his way in the fog."

"What's that noise?" Gertrude said. "What's that noise?" Caught in a swell, the raft rocked violently beneath us, and from somewhere ahead we could hear an angry slap-slap of waves.

"Well, it's not a reef or anything," Hunter said.

"I wish it were."

Arthur said, "Mrs. Otterdale. Miss Harrison! Let go my hands!"

"I'm frightened."

"I must retain my freedom of action."

The raft now rocked continuously. Almost without noticing it, we had moved forward along the deck to stare into the fog ahead of us, and now were grouped along the edge. We could see that the water was rough with waves that chopped and slapped at one another like disturbed bath water, though on a rather larger scale. Foam broke on the crests of these waves, shining through the weed that lay everywhere about the surface. Another fish leapt from the water, and landed on the deck between us. It was followed into the air by a long grey body with grasping tentacles; this, baulked of its prey, dropped back again into the sea. Gertrude screamed. "Snakes!" she cried. "Snakes!" and clutched at Arthur.

"It's only a squid," Hunter said.

Arthur said, "Go inside, ladies."

"I can't," Muriel said. "If I can't see, I don't know what I won't imagine."

"Can't go in," Gertrude said, "don't make us go in." She moaned again, as new life disturbed the water.

We were carried onwards, rocked and buffeted by this miniature storm. We had been too long becalmed. I said, "I'm beginning to feel ill. I'm sorry." Sonya said, "Oh God!" and moved away, and Arthur said, "Lean over the edge if you want to be sick, Mr. Clarke."

Now the long overture was over. We had become involved in something bigger than CinemaScope, Cinerama, or Todd-AO. The mists moved apart like a gauze curtain, and in the diffused light of the sun, the sea exploded into life. The whole natural cycle of hunt and be hunted was taking place before us at once. Tiny fish, which had come to feed on the weed and whatever organisms lived in it, were themselves pursued by larger fish, which were pursued by the squid, which were pursued by larger fish yet. They filled not only the surface of the water, but the air above the surface, and we saw, I will swear, fish that ate and were eaten in the space of a single leap. *Thump, thump* went the fishes on the deck of the raft. Little squid, the size of a hand, flew through the air like gulls. Porpoise and marlin broke water and submerged, their bodies gleaming like Baby Austins. And the fish screamed; I do not know the cause—whether trapped air was expelled from envelopes in their bodies or whether fish do indeed communicate in this way—but to us it seemed that they screamed, a thin shrill sound like boiling lobsters in a pot, mixed with a deeper grunting sound and with the foaming and slap of the waves.

To this noise the women added. There are those to whom a bat in the hair, a mouse running up the leg, are the end of terror. Could such a one imagine herself wearing a squid like a stole, its tentacles draped for a moment across her back and shoulders, its discharge of black ink discolouring her skin? It did not help Gertrude that Hunter shouted at her, "They're harmless. It's all right; they're quite harmless." She screamed, and kept on screaming. "Arthur!" she cried again and again, "Arthur! Save me, Arthur! You promised," until Muriel, whose jealousy overmastered her own fear, pulled off the squid, and struck at her, shouting, "He's mine. You're not to. You keep off him."

Sonya had backed against the cabin wall, and stood there stiffly, holding her hands over her belly to protect it; the child (if it were mine) would now be almost six months old. I felt sick, but felt also that I should be with her. I stumbled towards her, and the lurching of the raft flung me against the wall by her side. "Can't you leave me alone without bashing into me?" she shouted above the noise. "You know I only want to be left alone." I looked for Tony. He was with Hunter, filling buckets and pots with the fish that fell on the deck.

Muriel and Gertrude were on their knees now by Arthur, tugging at his blanket. I returned to the edge of the raft to be sick. One of the silly waves broke over my legs. It was ice cold, and, with the surprise, I almost slipped, and would have fallen overboard. "It's cold," I shouted, "it's cold." Nobody took any notice. I made my way to Arthur, and bellowed at him, "The water's gone cold. It used to be warm, and now it's icy." "Mr. Clarke, Mr. Banner," Arthur said. "Get rid of these women."

Banner took Gertrude by the arm. "Come on," he said. "Come on," and pulled. But Gertrude shook him off, and Muriel scratched my cheek when I tried to grasp her. "You're God," she shouted to Arthur. "You're God. You told us. Make it stop." I said, "Don't be silly. He didn't mean us to take him seriously," but Muriel cried, "God! God! Make it stop," and soon Gertrude joined in.

"Let go your hands then," Arthur said. "Take your hands from my robe."

The two women stopped clutching at the blanket, although they remained kneeling, resting their hams on the backs of their legs. Arthur indicated to Banner that we should kneel also, and we did. He seemed to think that this was enough. Holding the ends of the blanket in his hands, he spread his arms like wings, stood for a while with his wings spread, and then folded them forwards. "By virtue of the powers vested in me as God," he said, "I command you to stop." Nothing happened. Arthur spread his wings to the side again, and flapped them commandingly. "Waters!" he said. "Stop this nonsense. I command it." At once the fog closed in on us again. Whether it absorbed the sound, or whether the sound itself had ceased I do not know, but certainly we could no longer hear the fish screaming. "Go forth, and feel the water, Mr. Clarke," Arthur said, "and tell me also what you see there." I leaned over the edge of the raft while Banner held my legs. There was still plenty of weed, but the fish no longer enlivened it. The little waves were less violent; I had to wait before one came along that was high enough to wet my hand. "It's warm again," I said. "We're back to normal." "God be praised," Banner said, hauling me back. I nudged him sharply. "God Arthur be praised, that is," he said. Arthur allowed his blanket wings to fall again from his shoulders like a robe. "We shall go in now," he said. "There is nothing more to do here."

By next morning there was no sign of the place where the currents had met, and we were becalmed in bright sunlight as before. But among the fish that swam in around and beneath the raft, we saw for the first time the broad jaws and triangular fins of sharks and the little striped pilot fish that led them in their search for food.

11. Climax

"Harold?"

"Yes?"

"Do you want a game?"

"Can't. I've got to take the god his lunch."

"I'll wait then."

"All right."

We had drawn out a draughts board and a halma board with charcoal on the deck of the raft. Gertrude and Banner spent much time in playing. They used Glub Cushions for men, and kept a running score in blurred charcoal marks, over which they argued frequently.

Muriel was singing: *"Root them up. Put them behind. Four little foxes that will spoil the vine. Envy, jealousy, malice, pride; All if allowed will in your heart abide."* She had a great store of such songs, and would croon for hours to herself, *Wide, Wide as the Ocean* or *I'm H.A.P.P.Y.* or *Lonesome Valley* or any of a dozen others that I cannot now remember. Sonya also sang as she sat in the shade, swollen and heavy in her pregnancy, and the different words and tunes would cut across each other and interweave in gentle disharmony.

The god Arthur remained within the inner cabin. The men slept on the open deck, the women had our former sleeping quarters, and the god Arthur lived permanently in the bedroom of the raft; it had become his temple. Only Banner, who was now the priest of the god Arthur, was allowed to see him, and Banner prepared his food, though I continued to cook for the rest. The quarto volumes of the raft's log had been taken into the temple, and were now the Sacred Books, and in the main cabin a candle and the god Arthur's old yellow oilskins had been grouped together to make an altar. When we gathered together round the cabin table for supper, Banner would light the candle, and place the god Arthur's portion on this altar as an offering; then we would all turn our backs while he carried it into the next room. No particular ritual was yet associated with the god's washing-up; his plate was washed with the others by the women.

"Flow gently," Sonya sang. "Flow gently, sweet Afton," and Tony, to whom she was teaching the song, echoed, her, "Sweet Afton".

"Flow gently, sweet Afton, Among thy green braes. . . ."
". . . green braes."
("Put them behind—" from Muriel.)
"Flow gently. I'll sing thee, A song in thy praise."
"Four little foxes that will spoil the vine."
"My Mary's asleep, By thy murmuring stream. . . ."
". . . stream."
"Envy, jealousy, malice, pride. . . ."
"Flow gently, sweet Afton. Disturb not her dream. . . ."
"All if allowed will in your heart abide."
". . . abide."
"No, dream."
"Dream."

I moved away, and went to sit by Hunter. I was in a dream of tigers. I could not talk to Sonya any more; I could not talk to Tony. Sometimes during these days after the meeting of the currents, I would find myself shivering violently; sometimes my voice would play tricks, hovering and changing like a boy's, breaking when I was nervous into a bronchial falsetto. I became furtive. I would hang about the fringes of a conversation, my glance sliding over the faces of the speakers, holding no one's gaze. For a while I would force myself to behave sensibly; when the strain of this became too great, I would retire into the private jungle of my tigers until restlessness drove me to look for company. Sonya, although she could not share my feelings, knew that something was wrong, and was sorry for it. Once she came over (although more often she would avoid me) and laid her head against my shoulder, but neither of us took the chance to speak, and nothing was gained but a moment's peace. At other times, because she was herself worried and frightened, she would snap at me. "You'll only begin to twitch if you hold yourself tense all the time," she said, and I did fancy afterwards that a nerve leapt independently from time to time at the corners of my mouth.

Banner appeared. "The god Arthur wants some glue," he said.

"Flow gently, sweet Afton, among thy green——?"

"Braes."

"Braes. Flow gently. I'll sing thee a song in thy praise."

"That's right, Tony. Now let's try to get the tune."

"What's he want glue for?"

"He didn't say."

"It is better not to question the god's desires," Gertrude said. "Whatever the god wants is good. Perhaps he has a use for glue. Perhaps——" her voice took on a more reverent tone— "Perhaps he just wants it."

"I think there's some glue with the tools in the hold. I'll go and get it."

"No, I'll go," Banner said. "Otherwise it would only have to be purified."

Gertrude said, "Now we'll miss our game. But of course the service of the god must come first."

"I'll give you a game if you like," I said.

"We'll have to keep a separate score then."

"I don't mind if there isn't a score at all."

"Oh, we have to keep a score. There's no point in playing if you don't remember who's won."

"Try again, Tony," Sonya said.

"My Mary's asleep by——?"

"Thy mur——"

"Mur——"

"—muring stream. . . ."

"Can't you shut up singing that?" I said. "It only puts me off."

"Envy, jealousy, malice, pride."

Gertrude said, "You have to take me." She moved her man over four of my Glub Cushions, and swept them off the board, saying, "You're not very good, are you?"

"I can't concentrate with Tony caterwauling all the time."

All if allowed will in your heart abide.

Banner came up from the hold, carrying a large brown paper bag. "I'm not sure whether this is gum arabic or another sort of Glub," he said.

"Gum arabic."

"I'll take it in then."

Gertrude said, "We'd better try halma. You're not much good at draughts."

"I don't feel like it."

"John," Gertrude said. "Don't struggle. The god Arthur is good and necessary. Why don't you accept the truth as we do, and then you will feel right with yourself."

"That's right," Banner said, reappearing. "Just make an act of faith. Everything follows from that."

"You'll be a different man."

"I don't want to be a different man."

"Don't you? Are you so happy as you are?"

"What does he want with the glue?"

"He wants me to make a mask," Banner said. "The women can help. We soak paper in the glue, and it turns into papier mâché. Then we mould it, and it hardens."

"What does he want a mask for?"

"He says his face is too terrible for us to see."

"You see it."

"Not lately. He's been putting his head under the sheet. I think he's growing a beard. He says we're to make eyeholes and a mouth. He says this is going to be a smiling mask, but later on we may have to make a frowning one."

"Oh, Harold," Gertrude said, "I hope he will never appear to us in a frowning mask."

"Not to us," Muriel said. "But he may to some."

They boiled the gum in a pot with sea water, soaked pages from *Britain's Beauty Spots* in it, and made a sort of papier mâché. There was enough for both a smiling and a frowning mask, so both were made; Gertrude sketched in the features, which had a strong flavour of the Greek theatre. Banner told us that the god Arthur was pleased with the masks, and soon we should be allowed to enter the temple, and hold communion with him—"when his beard's grown, I expect," Banner said.

In fact, the god's beard was rather strange. It was sparse, and grew in a fringe round the edges of the mask; he looked like a Mormon playing Oedipus. Also, since not even Banner was allowed to give the god the kind of basin haircut we gave each other, he had become shaggy. We had little chance, however, to observe the details of the god's appearance closely at this time, because we had to keep our heads bent in reverence. Speaking from behind the mask, the god Arthur sounded as though he had no roof to his mouth. "Ha ha ha hee ho hi," he said, and Banner translated. "The god tells us that soon we shall see great things. He has a surprise for us."

The air in the cabin was close and hot. There was the stench of sweat, both ours and the god's, for I do not think he had been washing very much; I suppose he did not care to risk meeting any of us in the bathroom. I realized for the first time that it wasn't any fun being the god Arthur, and that Arthur, however deluded by self and circumstance, was sacrificing himself for us. Sonya moaned suddenly, and fell down in a faint. "Hee ha hee ho ho ho," said the god Arthur, and Banner said, "She has been overcome by the nearness of the god." Immediately Muriel fainted also.

Tony and I carried Sonya out into the air. There were deep pools of sadness below her eyes under the tan; she looked small and afraid. "What's going to become of me?" she said, "Johnny, I'm frightened."

I motioned to Tony to go away, and he did. "I'll help," I said. "It's not anything to . . . native women . . . they just go off into the bushes. They don't need doctors or anything." She gripped my hand tightly. I said, "We'll all help. Both the women."

"Not Muriel."

"No, not Muriel. I'll keep her away. Gertrude'll help you. And it's not for a month or so yet. We'll find land before then. There'll be . . . oh, all sorts of people."

"No, there won't." There was a long silence. "It doesn't matter really." Sonya did not let go my hand. "We won't let her be a dancer whatever happens. There's no future in it," she said.

Banner came fussing out. "Has she recovered? Is she all right?" He had removed his vestments; that is to say he had taken off the made-over sheet that the god Arthur required him to wear over his trunks. "I expect she was seized," he said. "You often hear of such cases in the United States. And in the Bible too, of course."

"I expect so."

"The spirit, you know."

"I expect so."

"Muriel has been frothing. It is most impressive."

"You'd better go and look after her then."

When Banner had gone inside the cabin again, I said gently to Sonya, "I won't be so foolish. I know he's really mine. I know when it was too. It was that time at Chew Magna. He'll be born out of . . . out of love, Sonya; that's always an easy birth. I love you. You know that. I won't be stupid any more."

But Sonya was asleep, and could not hear me, and even as I watched over her, sleeping gently with her head on my lap in the shade of the cabin, even as I looked down at the sharp bones of her face and her swollen belly that stood out all the more prominently from her wasted body, even as tenderness and compassion and all those parts of love that I had for so long stifled swept over me in a flood, the old jealousies returned with the tenderness, and I began again to question and to wonder.

*   *   *

Muriel's fit was a great score for her. She said she had been possessed. "I'm afraid she may bear fruit," Banner said. "You must see how this undermines my position."

Gertrude said, "It isn't fair. Aren't I the god's hand-maiden too?" She took it very ill, and spent much time mooning on deck, staring at the water, and sucking her thumb. I suggested that she might become possessed as well. "Oh, if only there were that possibility," she replied, and I thought at our next communion with the god that I saw her begin to quiver in preparation, but Muriel forestalled her. "I don't think Muriel ought to be possessed every Sunday afternoon," I said. "It's sort of suburban."

Shortly after this, the god Arthur demanded first fruits. For the time being, the first fruits were fish. Banner would carry Hunter's first catch of the day into the temple, and the god would decide whether to have it for lunch or order it to be thrown to the sharks. The fish had to be caught; none of the flying fish that fell on deck during the night would do. They were a great nuisance, and a hazard to the sleepers; Banner especially would awake with a shout when one landed on him.

Banner had become touchy, first with having his new position, and then with not being sure of it. He and Muriel began to get into arguments. Muriel said that, since she had been possessed by the god and might give birth at any moment, she ought to have preferential treat-ment and special food. Banner pointed out that Sonya was also an expectant mother, and much nearer her time. Muriel said that it was not at all the same thing. Whoever was the father of Sonya's child—and she looked wickedly at me—he was not a god. Tony said, "Sometimes I wish there was chips with this fish," and the conversation took another turn.

We caught a shark. It was Hunter's decision. He said, "Going to catch a shark today. Come and help."

The time was about ten o'clock in the morning. The sea was as clear and as still as usual; the sharks kept their usual station. Hunter said he had heard that pork was the proper bait, but we would have to use another fish, gutted so that it bled. The bait was taken almost at once, and we four men hauled the shark in while the women gave little cries of encouragement. We kept a good deal of line between the shark and ourselves, and we watched from a distance as it flapped and writhed on deck. Muriel said, "They've only got to touch you with their teeth, you know. You can see how sharp they are. You could lose a leg."

Tony said, "There was some kids stoned a cat to death in the bomb site near where we lived."

Sonya said, "Did you help?"

"No. But I watched. I was only twelve. When it was nearly dead, one of the kids went to bash its head with a stone, and it got him. His hand went septic after."

We kept well away from the dead shark for most of the morning, just in case. When we were sure it was safe to approach, we discovered that we had no idea what to do with it. Banner said, "Shark steaks. Rather like chicken, I believe, if properly cooked." But Muriel didn't fancy that, and neither, we decided, did the rest of us, so we pushed the dead shark back into the water, and the other sharks ate it, having no such scruples.

Fighting broke out between Muriel and Gertrude after supper that night.

We had passed the most unpleasant period of our gastronomic history; there was no more raw fish. By experimenting with different kinds of fish, by broiling and boiling and steaming and frying and baking in the ashes of the fire, by varying the quantities of Glub and seawater, I managed to prevent our supper menus from becoming monotonous; "Surprise us," Sonya had said in the early days, and so I had, and surprised myself as well. For this evening I had prepared flying fish, fried crisp until you could eat the bones. Muriel looked at them with disrelish. "The god doesn't care for flying fish," she said.

Gertrude said, "How do you know?"

"He never has them for his first fruits."

"He has what we catch. We never catch flying fish. They catch themselves."

"The god doesn't like them."

"You're not an authority on what the god likes and doesn't like. Just because you say you've been possessed, that doesn't make you an authority."

Muriel did not reply.

Banner came out of the temple. "Well," he said, "the god has been pleased to accept our little offering, and now we can all tuck in."

"You see? He does like them."

"He respects our feelings."

"The god doesn't have to respect our feelings. He doesn't think about them. We're supposed to respect him and his feelings. If he didn't like flying fish, he'd throw them back. Isn't that right, Harold?"

"Well——"

Muriel said, "I don't pay any mind to you. You're only jealous."

"What have I got to be jealous about?"

"Because the god possesses me."

Gertrude said, "I was possessed a long time before you were, if you want to know. The god possessed me before he was a god."

"He was always a god. We didn't know it before."

"Well then."

"Well then what?"

"He was a god when he possessed me then."

"He never possessed you."

"I know whether I was possessed or not."

Banner had been making little ineffectual movements of

pacification, but he was hampered by his sheet. "Ladies, ladies!" he said.

"Why do you let her walk all over you, Harold?"

"I don't pay any mind," Muriel said. "Jealous bitch!"

Gertrude picked up a flying fish with her fingers. She leaned across the table, and slapped Muriel in the face with it. The fish was so crisp and brittle that it broke at once into pieces. I said, "You see? I said you could eat the bones." Muriel picked up a cup.

"No," Banner said, "don't throw anything. I'll tell the god." The cup missed Gertrude, and was shattered against the cabin wall.

Gertrude pushed back her chair, and stood up. I said, "For goodness' sake, hold on to them."

Tony said, "I don't like to." Muriel stood up also.

"Harold!"

"Ladies! Ladies!"

Gertrude said, "I've some pride left, Harold. I won't be insulted in front of all of you. I've had a lot of cruelty and inconsiderateness to put up with in my life—" she was shaking, and had to hold on to the table for support— "Parts that should have come to me have been given to someone else, because I've always told people what I thought, and never pretended. I've sat alone in a tiny room, waiting for the telephone to ring. I've made myself ask for favours sometimes; I've eaten dirt, and been refused. I've watched my own pupils pretend not to see me in the foyers of theatres. I've been ignored in the street."

"Now, Gertrude."

"This woman. What right has she to insult me? She falls down in a fit, and calls it possession."

"That'll do from you," Muriel said. "You keep your place. If the god prefers me to you, then you ought to take your medicine and keep quiet about it, instead of——"

Gertrude launched herself across the table, and stabbed with a fork at Muriel's stomach. But the distance was too great for her, and only one of the tines of the fork penetrated Muriel's skin, while Gertrude herself landed with her face in a plate. Muriel gazed at the single drop of blood raised by the wound. "I'm bleeding," she cried. Gertrude recovered, and put herself in position for another attack, but Muriel, crying, "I'm bleeding. You bitch, I'm bleeding," left her place, and came around the end of the table to grapple with her.

She had not even paused to arm herself with cutlery. She seized Gertrude's wrist, and twisted it until the fork dropped to the floor. Gertrude bit Muriel's shoulder. Muriel howled, and pulled Gertrude's hair with both hands. I moved protectively towards Sonya's chair, and so did Tony. "Ladies! Ladies!" Banner said again. The door of the temple opened, and Arthur came into the cabin.

He was wearing neither his frowning nor his smiling mask. His beard had been cut, and his hair combed; his spectacles glittered. His voice dominated the confused noises of the fighting women. "Mrs. Otterdale! Miss Harrison!" he said, "Stop it at once, and behave."

Muriel and Gertrude rolled apart; their faces were scratched and bleared with tears. Gertrude was the first to recover. She curtsied, and said as steadily as she could, "I'm sorry, god Arthur. The woman provoked me."

"I am not the god Arthur," Arthur said. "The god Arthur has gone back to heaven. I am the god Arthur born man."

In the silence, Banner began to pick up the broken pieces of the cup Muriel had thrown, and put them on the table. We moved back to our places, keeping our eyes lowered. Muriel stepped on the pieces of fish with which Gertrude had struck her, and they made a loud crunching sound.

Arthur took his place before the altar. "You can take off that silly sheet," he said to Banner, "I shall be the god's high priest from now on."

Life went on. The inner cabin continued to be used as a temple, and only the high priest Arthur was allowed to enter it. First fruits were still offered to the god Arthur, and the whole of our evening meal was placed on his altar to be blessed before being distributed among us. The first fruits themselves were now cast into the sea. High priest Arthur would put on his vestments, walk briskly to the edge of the raft, lift the dish in the air, say, "God Arthur be pleased to accept these first fruits," and into the water the fish would go. The gift was always accepted.

In the evenings, the high priest Arthur would often read to us from the Sacred Books. These had been much rewritten since he had first begun to enter up the log; indeed, he would often make alterations in the manuscript as we went along. I am sure that the first sentence of the log did not originally read, "In the beginning the god Arthur came out of the great rain," but that was how it read now. Mixed in with this sort of apocryphal statement, there were still traces of the old Arthur. "The god spoke to the people about the functions of rational man," he had written, and followed it with a string of Arthurisms; there was also a long piece about the god's concern with sanitation when it should have pleased him to bring us safely to land, and a discussion of the value of *tabu* in maintaining standards of cleanliness. His account of the storm was very highly coloured. "There came a great wind over the surface of the waters," it ran, "and the face of the sky was blackened by the waters, and the voice of the god was heard in the wind, crying 'Woe, woe to the sons of men', and many of those who were not of the Chosen were swallowed up by the waters, but the god held over the Chosen the shield of his hand, and all save one were saved." (Here the high priest paused, and continued reading on a different note) "Tidal waves have, of course, been known from the earliest times, and have done great damage to life and property. There is a natural explanation of their occurrence, having to do with the activity of underwater volcanoes, but never before have tidal waves followed each other in so long a series, and in this was the hand of the god shown." (He wrote in a sentence.) "In any case, the god would have created the volcanoes in the first place, being the prime mover of all things." The high priest looked up from his reading, and said to us, "Thus we may see that the god Arthur may appear, either, as in this case, as the immediate cause, or, as in the case of most other natural phenomena, as the ultimate cause, but cause he must be, and is."

The Sacred Books are lost now (I think Harold burned them), so I do not know how Arthur described the night of the squid. We had seen squid before, of course. Indeed, I had once tried to cook one in its own ink by a recipe only partly remembered from Elizabeth David's *Mediterranean Cooking*; it had turned out to be one of the dishes Muriel did not fancy. But we had never seen a squid like this.

Let me remember the date; it was on October 24th, and Sonya was within a month of her time. Though the weather was still warm, the evenings were shorter now, and supper had turned into high tea, for we continued to eat a little before sunset. The sea was calm, and the only happening out of the ordinary was that Hunter reported that all the fish seemed to be swimming in the same direction. We thought little of this, and ate our meal indoors as usual. Arthur read to us for a while from the Sacred Books. Then we went out on deck into the dusk to take the air.

We saw that the sea was no longer smooth. It looked like cobblestones. The water was covered with squid, little squid, harmless squid, cuttle-fish that we had caught and tried to cook, but now blanketing the surface of the sea all around us in the dusk. Many of them were eaten by the fish that their presence in such large numbers had attracted, so that it was as if the cobblestones were under a mock shell-fire; wherever we looked, we could see them seeming to disintegrate in a swirl and flash of foam, yet the surface remained unchanged, and there were always as many cobblestones as before. The sight was fascinating, but not frightening. Gertrude said, "It's almost as if you could step on them, and walk to land."

We remained on deck for a long time, watching the squid. Dusk thickened into night. The moon rose in a clear sky, and the bodies of the squid gleamed, a silver-grey in the moonlight, and we sat there, silently watching.

"But this is ridiculous," Arthur said. "It is past your bedtime. There is nothing to see."

"Please."

"Oh, you may stay if you wish."

In the silence we could hear each splash and gulp quite clearly. A little thread of wind came up, a little cold thread that seemed to pass from one to another of us, and then die. Sonya shivered. I put my arm around her shoulders, and felt her stiffen for a moment before relaxing within its warmth.

I said, "A clock ought to strike or something."

"Why?"

"I don't know. It's as if we were waiting for something to begin. Don't you feel that?"

"We are always waiting, Mr. Clarke. We should be waiting and ready at all times to do the god's will."

A long black serpent uncoiled from the water close to the raft, rose for a moment in the air, regarded us, and then returned to the water.

We did not speak. I think each of us felt that as long as we kept silent, we might be able to believe that we had seen some private hallucination, and there would be nothing. The serpent reappeared, and was joined by another. In the moonlight, we could see that the surface of their skins was not smooth, but rough and indented like tentacles. Gertrude said breathlessly, "Lord Arthur, tell them to go away".

The serpents fell back into the sea. Arthur said, "I must consult . . . I must ask. . . ."

Muriel said, "Tell the god to make them go away."
Sonya turned her head in to my shoulder, and I could feel that she was shaking, and hear the tiny chattering of her

teeth. One of the serpents began delicately to explore the edge of the deck.

Banner said, "High priest Arthur, please exorcise the demons before they eat us." None of us had raised his voice at all up to now, but Gertrude said, "I'm going to scream. I can feel it inside me. Please do something, Arthur, before I scream, because if once I start, I don't think I shall be able to stop."

There was a disturbance on the surface of the water some way from the raft. The serpent on deck was whipped back like a fishing-line, and was seen to be part of a nest of serpents, clustering around the head of a sea creature which lay not more than sixty feet away. There were eight other serpents as well as the two we had already seen, but they were much smaller. They writhed above a hooked beak of a mouth, as the creature raised its head to look at us.

Banner said, "Medusa!"

"If I'd been turned to stone, I shouldn't feel so frightened."

"Arthur! Arthur!"

Hunter said, "It's a squid. A giant squid."

"Make it go away."

We could see the creature's body now. It must have been about twenty feet long, and perhaps six feet wide, tapering away to a tail from which sprouted two vestigial wings. It was longer than any squid we had ever seen, or could have imagined. One of its tentacles flicked again towards the raft, lay for a while on deck, and was joined by its mate, which vanished again almost at once below the waterline. The two tentacles found a purchase, and began to pull, and we felt the raft shudder and then move towards the squid.

"Arthur!"

But Arthur could do nothing. His body was rigid. Only his hands moved, and they seemed slowly to be pulling the squid towards us, just as it pulled us towards it.

"Arthur!"

The movement stopped. The squid had amused itself by playing for a while with the raft, but perhaps we were not texturally interesting enough to be sport for long. We saw again from a much closer range the great horned beak and the vacancy of an eye. All ten of the serpents writhed again, and then, as suddenly as it had appeared, the creature was gone. Slowly the tension ran out of us. Sonya stopped shivering. Banner cleared his throat. Only Arthur remained as rigid as before, staring at the place where the squid had disappeared.

"You'll talk to the god?" Muriel said. "You won't let it come back?"

Arthur turned slowly to look at her. "Woman," he said. "That was the god. And he will come again."

* * *

He would come again; he would come again.

When would he come? Arthur did not know.

What should we do when he came? Arthur did not say.

What did the god want beyond the worship and gifts he had already? Arthur could not tell.

"But it's only a squid," I said next evening after supper. "You heard Hunter say it was only a squid."

Arthur said, "The god can take many forms. He can take the form of a man or of a squid. But in any form he is terrible."

"You don't really believe in all that?"

Arthur lifted his hand, and slapped my face. It was not a slap to hurt; it was no more than an instinctive gesture of shock, but it told me how deeply Arthur did believe what he was saying. There was a silence. "You had better leave the room," he said, and I rose, and went out on deck.

Banner joined me there shortly afterwards. "He's very angry," Banner said. "He wants to see you in the temple. He says there's no place for blasphemers among the Chosen. You'd better tell him you're sorry."

"You think he'll have me thrown overboard?"

"Oh, I hope not."

I had tried to make a joke, but Banner took the words seriously. Now I found that I was afraid. Nobody questioned Arthur's decisions. If he were to decide to have me thrown overboard, then over I should go. Thinking of this, I became very frightened indeed. I wanted to say, "You wouldn't let him?" but I dared not, because I knew what the answer would be. When I am frightened, the tension in my throat makes it difficult for me to speak. "I'll . . . I'll tell him I'm sorry," I said at last.

"You'd better. It was a very foolish and wicked remark."

"I'll tell him."

Banner went indoors again. The high priest would let me know when he was ready to see me. The moon shone steadily on water which was clear again, for the little squid had long since dispersed. I stayed on deck, trying to collect my thoughts and my confidence. If I could stop myself shaking, if I could establish some sort of physical control, it would be a beginning. I wanted to make water, but the lavatory was indoors, and if I were to piss over the side, I might be caught doing so when they came to summon me to the high priest.

"You can come in now," Banner said, reappearing. I walked through the main cabin to the temple. They were all sitting round the table, watching me, but I would not look at them.

I knocked. There was no reply from within the temple. Banner said, "I think you'd better enter."

Arthur was wearing the frowning mask. I made a low obeisance, like a man in an Arabian Nights story. "I'm very sorry, god Arthur," I said, "I am truly sorry that I have sinned."

"Ha hee ho ho," said the god. High priest Arthur took off the mask, and the god went back to heaven. "The god speaks through me," he said. "The god is angry."

"I'm sorry."

"I have told you before, Mr. Clarke, that sorrow is of no practical use without the intention of amendment. The god has borne with your doubt for a long time. It is necessary at the beginning that there should be one among the Chosen to doubt and rebel, so that his chastisement by the god should be remembered by the people."

"I'm not rebelling."

"Not at the moment, no. Although even now I think that in your heart. . . . However, you are not to be blamed for that. You do no more in your way, Mr. Clarke, than we all do in ours; you express the will of the god. He has willed your fault, because he wills your expiation.

"Expiation?"

"Everything has come together in my mind, Mr. Clarke, since you asked that foolish question. *Do I believe?* That you should doubt my belief for a moment indicates that I have been at fault. Do we all believe? If we believe, do we believe strongly enough? Will we make a sign of our belief? Will we make a sacrifice to the god?"

I did not know where this was leading, but I was less frightened than I had been. If Arthur were to have me thrown overboard, it would be as a punishment, not as a sacrifice, so that whatever he intended to sacrifice, it was not I. I said, "We do make a sacrifice, high priest. We give our first fruits to the god."

"That is an act of devotion, not a sacrifice. It does not hurt us to give them. And yet . . . 'first fruits'. That fits the pattern also."

"What pattern?"

"When the god came out of the sea, what did he want? It was not clear to me then. Although I am close to the god, since I am part of him, born into mankind, his intentions may not always be clear to me, Mr. Clarke; I see that now. I did not know that he would . . . I had thought foolishly that I was the only incarnation, the only interpreter. But I was powerless, Mr. Clarke; it was the god himself."

"The god Arthur?"

"Yes, the god Arthur. But in another form."

"It could not have been. . . . There is no possibility that it was . . . an anti-god?"

"No. Or I should have prevailed. It was the god—made squid. When the god wishes me to know his intentions, Mr. Clarke, his revelation comes with the speed of lightning. I had one such moment when I struck you. It was all clear at once. First fruits. . . . The god's appearance in the likeness of a sea creature. . . . Expiation. . . . The delay in coming to land. . . . Your own reference to Iphigenia. . . ."

"A sacrifice?"

"Yes."

I gathered together all the courage I had. I was certain now that Arthur did not mean I was to be the sacrifice. And, even if I was wrong, at least my offer would make no difference. I said, "You wish to sacrifice me, Arthur? I am ready, of course, to do as the god wills."

"No. Not you."

"Later perhaps?"

"Perhaps."

I was sweating with a relief; a drop ran down my nose, and splashed on my chin. Arthur seemed to be waiting for me to say something else. What? Suddenly, it seemed to me, the sweat turned cold. I had been so concerned with my own fear that I had not asked myself the question which Arthur now waited to answer.

"Who then?"

Arthur chuckled. "Why do you ask?" he said. "It can make no difference. We are all equal in the eyes of the god."

"Of course. Of course."

"The mechanics of the thing may need a little arrangement. That is often the case in matters of religion, is it not?"

Was he trying to trap me? It seemed better not to answer.

"I may need your help."

Sonya! Now I could see his drift; now it was clear. He aimed at Sonya, and my punishment was to be trapped into helping him. Sweat broke out again all over my body, and fear was like a thin sword in my bladder. I said, "I have to go to the bathroom. I'm sorry."

"Return at once then."

They were all there, still sitting round the table in the main cabin. My demeanour as I came out of the temple must have seemed a testimony to the power of the god in punishing. I saw their faces—Muriel glad and Gertrude pitying, Harold righteous and Hunter vacant, Tony puzzled, and Sonya—I could not see Sonya's face at all; it was just a golden blur. I had to think; I had to think of something. I leaned over the basin of the water closet, and was sick. For as long as I dared I stayed there, but nothing happened in my mind but fear and fog. I came out, closed the door slowly behind me, and returned to the temple. I had to think of something.

Perhaps the two of us together . . . Arthur himself could not prevail against the two of us, standing together. Hunter and Tony would not help him to— A pregnant woman! Sonya's disability was our strength. Surely they would not harm a pregnant woman, even if the god himself were to order it.

"The pregnancy is much advanced," Arthur said.

"Yes," I would buy time. "Would it not be better to wait? Some of the others might feel——"

"They would feel nothing and know nothing. A sacrifice need not be public to be effective; only the will to give and the decision to receive are important. Later the others would be told. That is the god's will."

"But how could they not——?"

"The delivery will take place here in the temple. As the father, you may expect to be present. Later, we shall take the child——"

"The child?"

"An innocent life. Unblemished. For the god. The first-born of our new society. An offering, and an expiation."

The relief! I was filled with relief until it almost ran out of my ears. Not Sonya. Nobody would hurt Sonya. I was not to be tested, not to be required to fight for her.

Only the child. Nobody could ask me, nobody could expect me to fight, to risk both our lives—risk them? to lose them certainly—to lose both our lives for a child a few hours old, something without even a personality; nobody could do that. It would not be pleasant, certainly, to sacrifice the child, not be easy to explain to Sonya herself (here began the first disquiet), but it was not so bad, not so fearful; it could be borne. "She'd better not be told," I said. "We'll have to say it died or something."

"Naturally. It will be a secret we shall share with the god."

"Yes."

"You may go now, Mr. Clarke."

As I left the temple for the second time, I was not shaking, not sweating, not sick at the stomach. Only my face was flushed, my ears red; I felt a disinclination to talk to any of the others in the cabin. I walked straight past without looking at them, and went out on to the deck to be by myself for a while; I was beginning to wonder what I could say to Sonya, either now or in the future. Now that I thought I was alone, I raised my glance from the ground, and there was Tony, sitting in Hunter's fishing-seat, and staring thoughtfully at the water. He looked round as I approached. "Been chewing you up, has he?" he said. "It's a fair carry-on, isn't it?"

"Yes."

"He's funny—Arthur."

"I'm glad you think so."

"Well, you know—I mean, all this stuff. Being god and then not being god and all. You never know where you are with him."

"Don't you believe in it then?" I said slowly.

Tony grinned. I noticed for the first time how light and clear his eyes were. "Don't know much about it really," he said. "I mean, I can never tell what you're all talking about."

"But you always do what you're told. You never. . . ."

You've never attempted. . . . I'm the only one who's ever tried——"

"Well, he is the gaffer, isn't he?" Tony said. "I mean, you have to do what he tells you. He's clever, you know. I mean, all the things he thinks of. And it's not as if he did any harm with being a god and all. If that's what he likes, good luck to him."

"No harm? What about Wesley Otterdale?"

"You mean, like that Muriel thinks Arthur pushed him over?"

"Yes."

He grinned again. "She can think that if she wants to; she gets a kick out of it, I'd say. But Arthur was inside with us when Wesley went overboard; you know that. It was you let go of him, and he got washed away, wasn't it?"

"Yes."

"Well then?"

I was silent. "Look," Tony said, "I didn't say I didn't believe in it like."

"You said——"

"I said I didn't know. It's not my business, see? Religion and that, it's always been sort of—sort of above me, really. Not that I'd do anything wrong. I mean—" For the first time since I had known him, Tony was trying to explain a point of view. It was not easy for him, but he persisted. "Right and wrong," he said, "they've got a lot to do with religion, of course. Like murder's wrong, f'rinstance, only it would be wrong anyway, whether the Bible said so or not. And grassing on your friends, now, that's wrong, and the Bible doesn't say nothing about that at all. But adultery and that. Well, I mean, people do that all the time."

"Do they?" I said.

"Well, you know they do. I mean, you and Sonn—you aren't married."

It was as if he had broken a dam. All my guilt and self-doubt, which had been growing ever since I had fallen in so readily with Arthur's suggestion, were now added to the jealousy and suspicion that had already gone rotten inside me, and both came flowing out. I took three steps towards Tony, and laid one hand on his arm, thrusting my face close to his. "You should know, shouldn't you?" I said. "You should bloody well know."

"Eh?"

"You don't know anything about it, do you, you smug sanctified right-thinking bastard? Arthur and what he does to us, that's none of your business. You just do what's right. We can destroy ourselves up here. And as long as you do your bloody exercises every day, and f—— away to your heart's content in the hold——"

"What do you mean?"

"No, Sonya and I aren't married. So it's all right, isn't it? And even if we were married, it'd be all right because everyone does it, don't they? And I . . . I can't even kill you because I'm not strong enough. Maybe I ought to do some bloody exercises."

I was weeping quite freely now, and the tears ran down my cheeks, and splashed on Tony's bare shoulders. He stared at me, his mind taking in my meaning slowly, as it always did. "Me and Sonn?" he said. "Down there? What are you talking about?"

"You know what I'm talking about. Did you think I didn't know what you did down there? Everybody knew. The whole bloody lot of them knew. Muriel. Arthur. I heard them talking about it. Laughing. Just because we weren't— And you were bigger, so I couldn't do anything about it. I couldn't even prove it."

"Did Sonn say we——?"

"She wouldn't say you didn't."

"You fool!" Tony said. "You don't know nothing, do you?" He turned his face away from me, and looked out over the water. His voice was constrained. "I can't, if you want to know," he said, "I just can't. I haven't been able to for I don't know how long."

"You can't what?" I said. I had stopped weeping. "What do you mean—you can't?"

"I just can't; that's all. I don't know why it is. If it was anyone else, it'd be funny. I never used to be like this. The boys used to call me a sex maniac. It wasn't healthy. That's one of the reasons I took up body-building, see?—to take my mind off sex, like. And after a bit, it worked. I found I wasn't . . . interested no more. I thought it was the exercise done it, and being so tired when I come home from the gym. And then I won all them prizes, and had my picture on the cover of *Health and Strength*, and all the girls was after me, and then when I did want to, I just couldn't."

I began to feel foolish, and took my hand from Tony's arm. He kept his face averted from me, but even in the moonlight I could tell that he was blushing.

"I've tried," he said. "Over and over. They won't believe it at first. They think I must be queer or something. You know how it is with some of them photographers, always wanting you to strip off and all, but somehow I couldn't fancy that."

He seemed close to tears. I said, "I'm sorry, Tony."

"That's all right."

"I've been . . . I'm sorry."

"Being a father, I expect," Tony said, "it takes people funny ways. They talk about women getting fancies and all that, but I——"

"A father." All the tension went out of my legs, and I began to fall.

Tony caught me, and lowered me to the deck. "You all right?" he said.

"I don't think I can get up."

"You sick or something? I'll get Arthur."

"No." I sat there, looking at him. I felt rather liquid inside, but quite calm. I said, "Tony, will you help us get away?"

"Leave, you mean? You and Sonn?"

"Yes."

"Where to?"

"I don't know."

"You'll die. No food or nothing. What d'you want to leave for?"

"We have to. Arthur says the god needs a sacrifice. He says that's why it came out of the sea. He says it wants a life—something new and unblemished. He says that when Sonya's baby is born, I have to help him sacrifice it to the god."

"What did you say?"

"I said I would."

There was a long silence. "You must be bloody mad," Tony said, and went indoors.

He went straight into the temple. He didn't even knock. When Arthur saw him, he put on the frowning mask quickly. "Hee ha—" he said, and then Tony pulled it off him. "Bloody kids' stuff," Tony said.

Arthur reached behind the pillow of the bunk, and brought out a kitchen knife, sharpened at the point and at both edges; it was his sacrificial knife. With this he stabbed at Tony, cutting his shoulder. Tony put his hand to the wound, which was bleeding. "Christ!" he said. He reached out for Arthur, but Arthur dodged, and went backwards quickly through the door and into the main cabin. "Stop him," he said. "He is attacking the high priest."

Muriel began to move, but Tony said, "The first one that comes near me will get her face bashed in. This loony wants to kill little kids."

Arthur said, "Mr. Clarke had no right to say anything about it. He promised to tell nobody."

Tony said, "Well, he told me."

Everyone in the cabin remained where he was, and watched Tony and Arthur. Arthur still had the knife, and Tony did not try to look for a weapon, but kept his gaze on Arthur, and came steadily towards him. Arthur backed through the cabin door, and went out on deck. Tony followed him. On the bare deck, the two began to circle around one another.

As for me, I was still sitting there. All the strength seemed to have left me, and had been replaced by peace of spirit. I was quite content to watch. If Arthur were to kill Tony, I supposed I should have to fight. But I hoped that Tony would kill Arthur.

It seemed as if they would circle for ever. Whenever Tony lunged at Arthur, then Arthur would cut at him with the knife, and Tony would have to dodge. Arthur, on the other hand, did not dare to pass first at Tony, for fear that Tony would catch his wrist. "You will all be helpless without me," he said.

Nobody replied.

Tony was the heavier, but Arthur was the cleverer. He had manoeuvred Tony into a position in which Tony had the closer edge of the raft at his back. Slowly they approached that edge. I said clearly, "You'd better be careful, Tony, or you'll be over." For a moment, Tony relaxed his attention to glance behind him, and Arthur seized the opportunity to close.

He stabbed for the neck, but misjudged, and the blow went lower. In the bright moonlight, Tony's blood was black, staining his chest. He had caught Arthur's wrist, and the two struggled together, poised on the edge of the raft. Then they both fell into the water. There was a swirl and a snap, and a single shriek from Arthur, but the attendant sharks gave him no time for last words. Tony made no sound whatever.

I stood up, and went to Sonya. She said, "Tony! Poor Tony!" put her arms around my neck, and wept freely. I guided her gently indoors, and put her to bed in the temple, spending the night on the floor beside her bunk. The others slept on deck.

In the morning, Banner woke us. "You can see land ahead," he said. "I think it's an island. There are trees and everything."

And so we came to land at last, and to a land that was green, luxuriant and fruitful—the Promised Land of the New Society, Arthur would have called it, but we made no such speculations, and simply set about the business of keeping alive. Arthur's last words, "You will be helpless without me," were not justified by experience. We had been helpless with him, but without him we had to help ourselves.

It was as if our time on the raft had been a long process of recession. We had begun as ordinary, grown-up intelligent human beings, and slowly self-doubt, the habit of self-justification, jealousy, possessiveness, all the ordinary human faults had destroyed us. I myself with my tigers and my need to feel intellectually superior; Muriel with her special position, first as Arthur's spy and then as the woman possessed by the god; Hunter who had run away from any commitment to society before the Flood, and who continued to run away even from our small society on board the raft; Harold and Gertrude, whose ideals were vitiated by doubt and lack of purpose; even Sonya, whose candidness and trust my jealousies destroyed.

But Tony had not been worried by doubts. His horizons were not large; his ambitions were limited. He performed the simple discipline of his exercises; he gave to other people a wide tolerance and respect; he made no moral judgements outside the simple estimate of right and wrong that he applied to himself. Tony was not a noble savage. On the contrary, he fitted very well into a society, asking no more than that it should give him work to do, respect his privacy, and not require him to do anything that he believed to be wrong. He had the simplicity that we think of as childish, but on the raft it was the rest of us who had become as demanding as children, as parasitic, as spiteful, as uncertain. We had moved back, unknowing, making the long journey into childishness as, also without our knowing, the raft had been borne steadily along by the current towards the island.

When he went overboard, Tony left us an example, and by taking Arthur with him, he lifted from us an incubus. We have profited from both.